U.S. States and Territories Maps

Map Resource Book

Artist:	Pat St. Onge
Editor:	Mary Dieterich
Proofreader:	April Albert

COPYRIGHT © 2016 Mark Twain Media, Inc.

ISBN 978-1-62223-593-3

Printing No. CD-404248

Mark Twain Media, Inc., Publishers
Distributed by Carson-Dellosa Publishing LLC

Table of Contents

Introduction

Mark Twain Media's *U.S. States and Territories Maps* book provides you with high-quality maps and worksheets for use with geography and other social studies curriculum. Maps and blank worksheets are included for all 50 states and the five U.S. territories, as well as for the United States as a whole. Teachers, parents, and students will find this a valuable resource when studying the states and territories.

Each state and territory map is labeled with the state capital, major cities, major rivers, and other bodies of water. The surrounding states are also labeled. Each worksheet is blank, providing an opportunity for students to label the cities and physical features of the state.

These maps allow students to practice their geography skills. Use the maps with your own curriculum in a variety of ways to reinforce the five themes of geography: location, place, region, movement, and human-environment interaction.

All maps and worksheets are reproducible. They can also be made into transparencies or scanned and used digitally on computers, whiteboards, and other classroom projection devices. The e-book format is ready to use digitally, and the maps can be printed for classroom or individual student use.

Photo credit: USMC-071002-M-8077B-001.jpg {PD-USMC} 28 Sept. 2007. <http:www.marines.mil/unit/2ndmlg/PublishingImages/2007/071002-M-8077B-001.jpg> <https://commons.wikimedia.org/wiki/File:USMC-071002-M-8077B-001.jpg>

Name: _____

Date: _____

The Fifty States

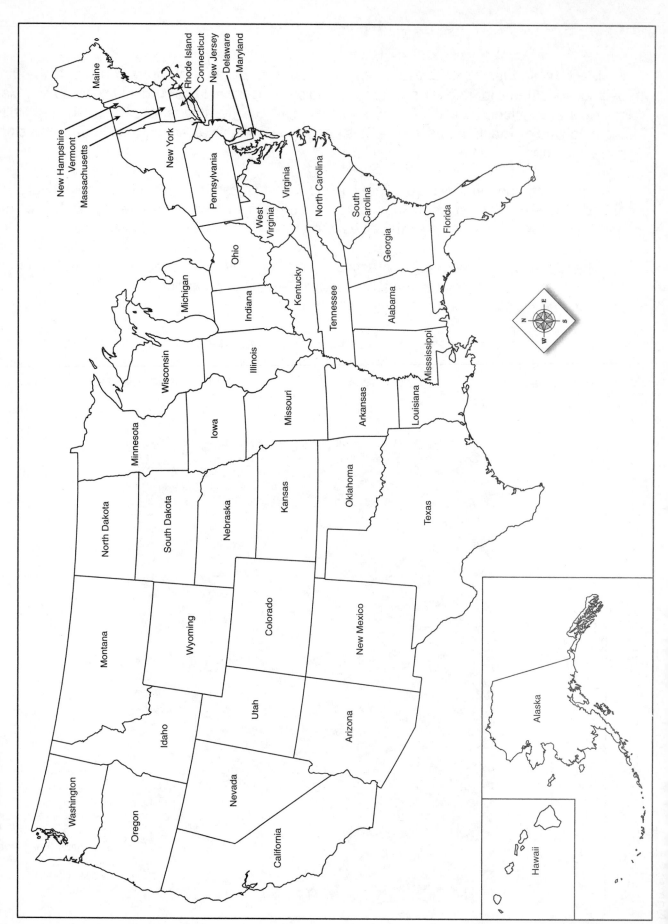

Name: _____

Date: _____

The Fifty States: Capitals and Postal Abbreviations

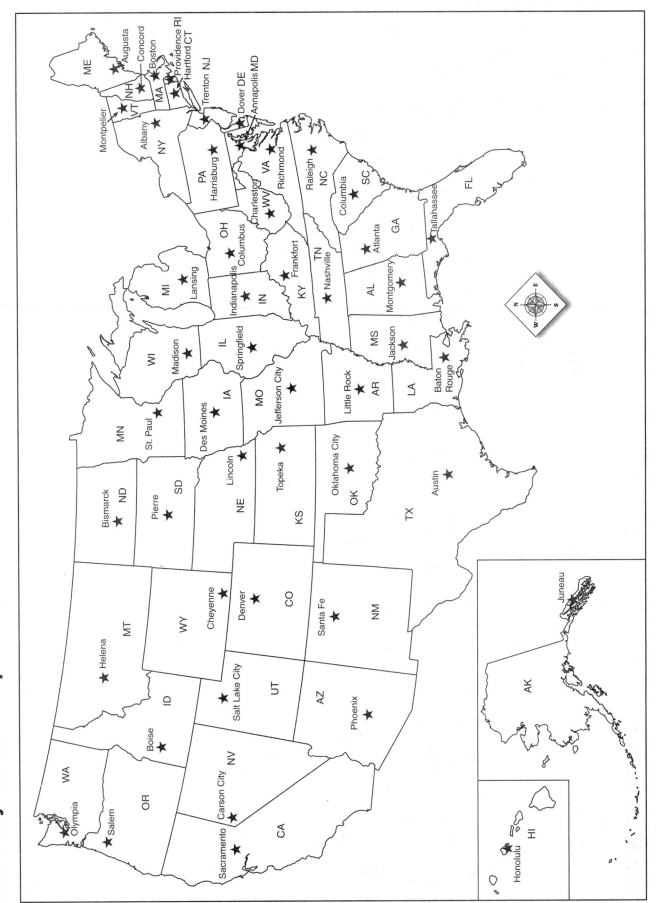

Name: _____

Date: _____

The Fifty States: Postal Abbreviations

Name:

Date: _____

The Fifty States: Blank

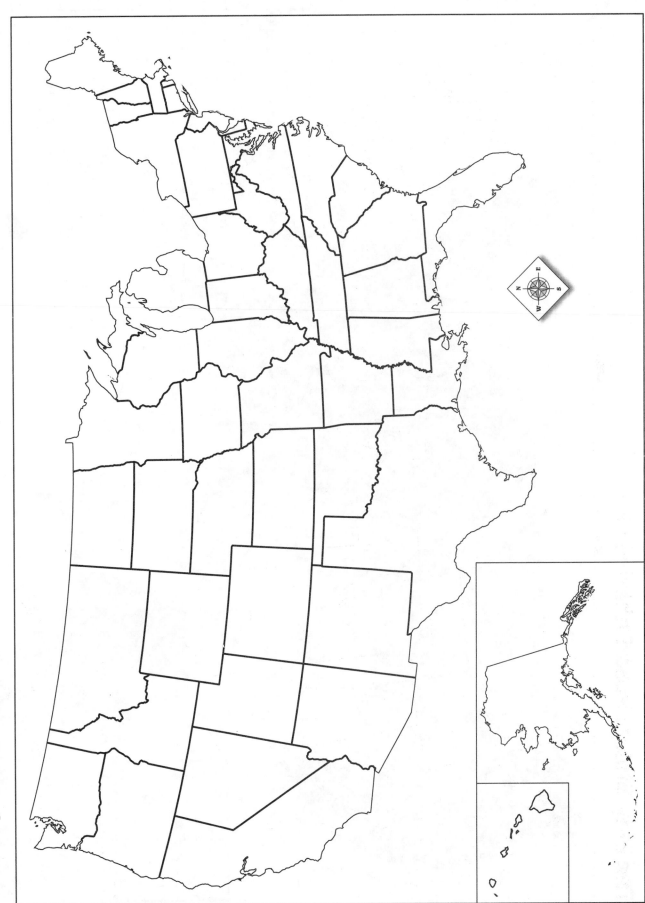

Name: _____

Date: _____

Regions of the United States

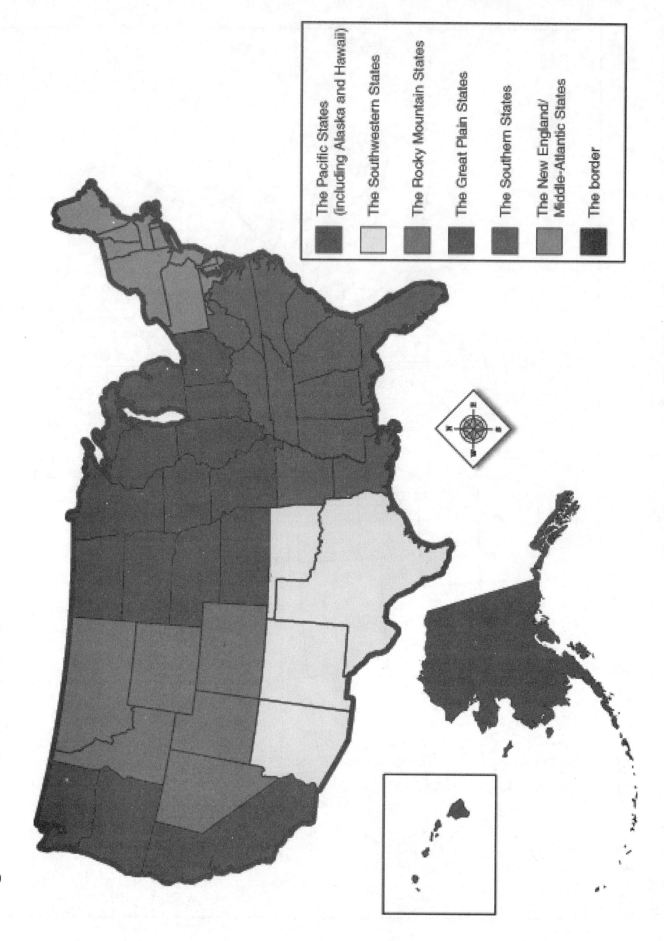

The Pacific States
(including Alaska and Hawaii)

The Southwestern States

The Rocky Mountain States

The Great Plain States

The Southern States

The New England/
Middle-Atlantic States

The border

Name: _____

Date: _____

Alabama

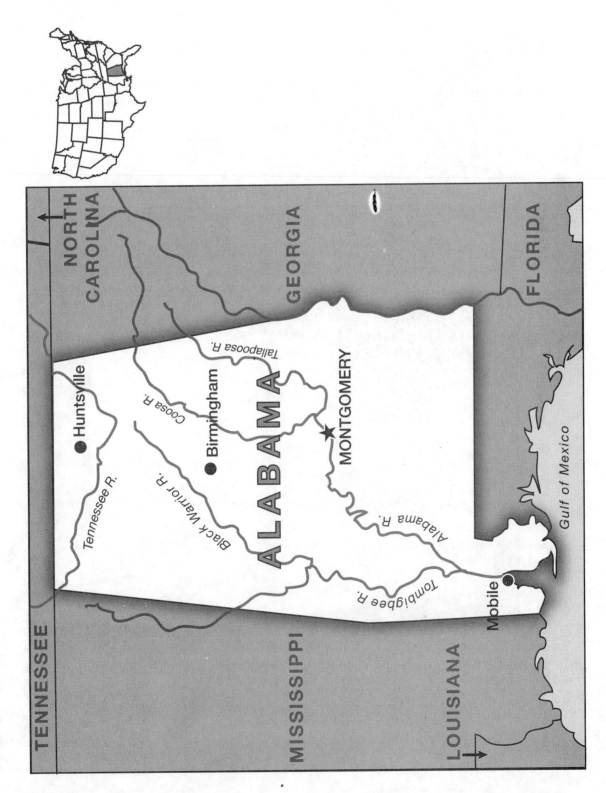

TENNESSEE

NORTH CAROLINA

MISSISSIPPI

GEORGIA

ALABAMA

LOUISIANA

FLORIDA

Gulf of Mexico

● Huntsville

Tennessee R.

Coosa R.

Black Warrior R.

Tallapoosa R.

● Birmingham

★ MONTGOMERY

Alabama R.

Tombigbee R.

● Mobile

Name: _____

Date: _____

Alabama Map Worksheet

Directions: Label the map with the following:
Cities—Birmingham, Huntsville, Mobile, Montgomery   Body of Water—Gulf of Mexico
Rivers—Alabama R., Black Warrior R., Coosa R., Tallapoosa R., Tennessee R., Tombigbee R.
States—Alabama, Florida, Georgia, Louisiana, Mississippi, North Carolina, Tennessee

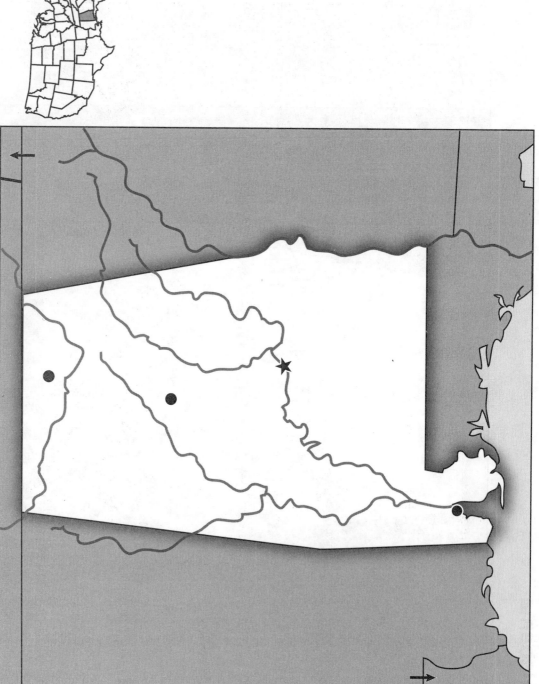

Name: _____

Date: _____

Alaska

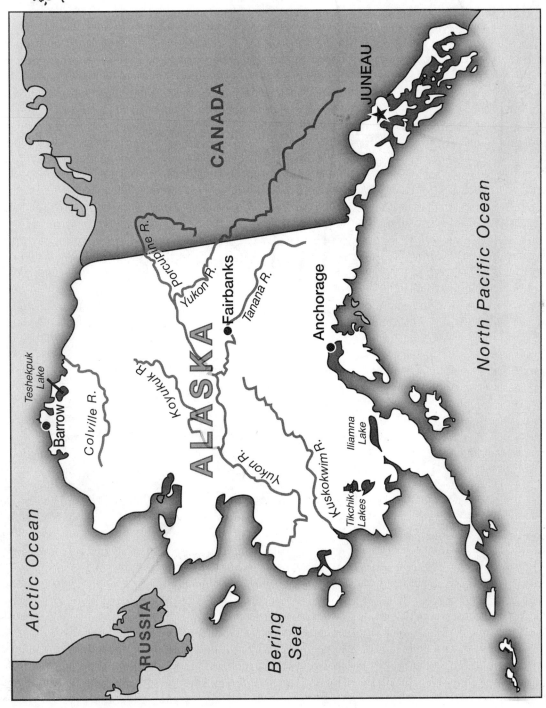

Arctic Ocean

RUSSIA

Bering Sea

North Pacific Ocean

CANADA

JUNEAU

ALASKA

Anchorage

Fairbanks

Barrow

Teshekpuk Lake

Colville R.

Koyukuk R.

Porcupine R.

Yukon R.

Tanana R.

Yukon R.

Kuskokwim R.

Tikchik Lakes

Iliamna Lake

Name: _____

Date: _____

Alaska Map Worksheet

Directions: Label the map with the following:

Cities—Anchorage, Barrow, Fairbanks, Juneau   States—Alaska   Countries—Canada, Russia
Rivers—Colville R., Koyukuk R., Kuskokwim R., Porcupine R., Tanana R., Yukon R.
Bodies of Water—Arctic Ocean, Bering Sea, Iliamna Lake, North Pacific Ocean, Teshekpuk Lake, Tikchik Lakes

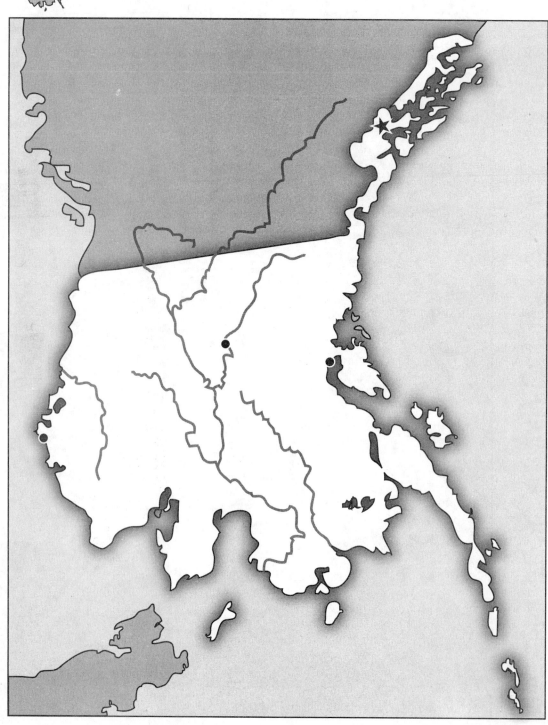

Name: _____

Date: _____

Arizona

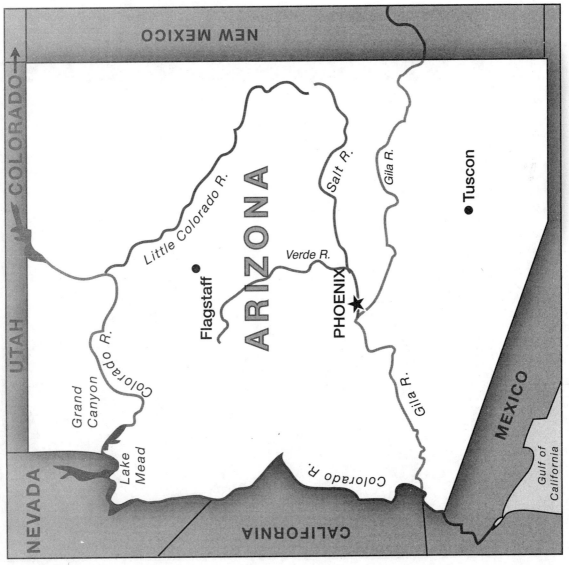

Name: _____

Date: _____

Arizona Map Worksheet

Directions: Label the map with the following:

Cities—Flagstaff, Phoenix, Tuscon

Rivers—Colorado R., Gila R., Little Colorado R., Salt R., Verde R.   Body of Water—Gulf of California

States—Arizona, California, Colorado, Nevada, New Mexico, Utah   Country—Mexico

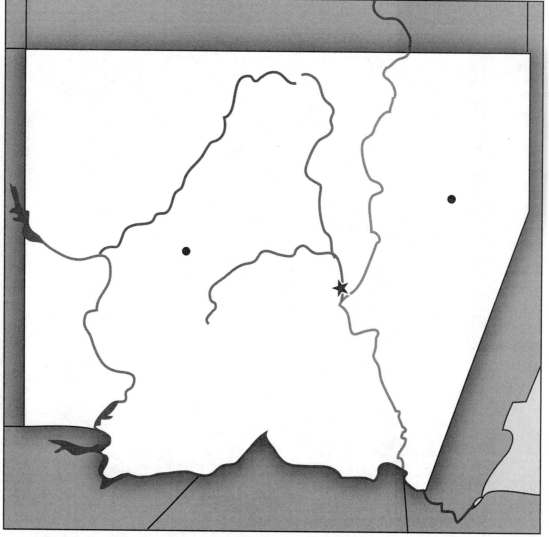

Name:

Date:

Arkansas

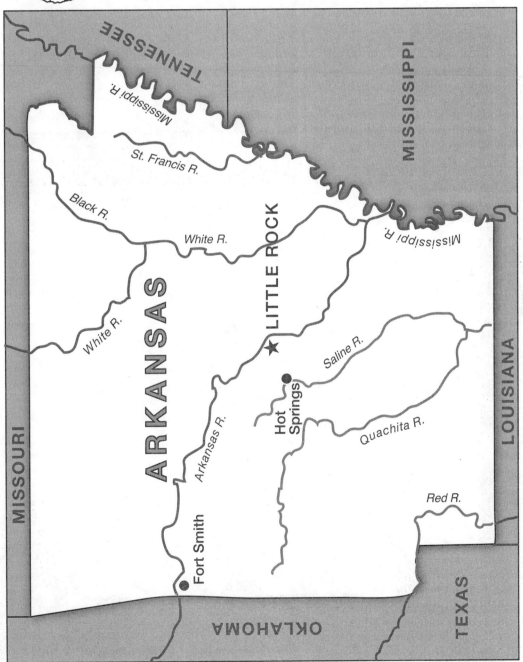

MISSOURI

TENNESSEE

MISSISSIPPI

Mississippi R.

St. Francis R.

Black R.

White R.

ARKANSAS

White R.

LITTLE ROCK

★

Mississippi R.

Saline R.

Arkansas R.

Hot Springs

Quachita R.

LOUISIANA

Fort Smith

Red R.

OKLAHOMA

TEXAS

Name: _____

Date: _____

Arkansas Map Worksheet

Directions: Label the map with the following:

Cities—Fort Smith, Hot Springs, Little Rock

Rivers—Arkansas R., Black R., Mississippi R., Quachita R., Red R., Saline R., St. Francis R., White R.

States—Arkansas, Louisiana, Mississippi, Missouri, Oklahoma, Tennessee, Texas

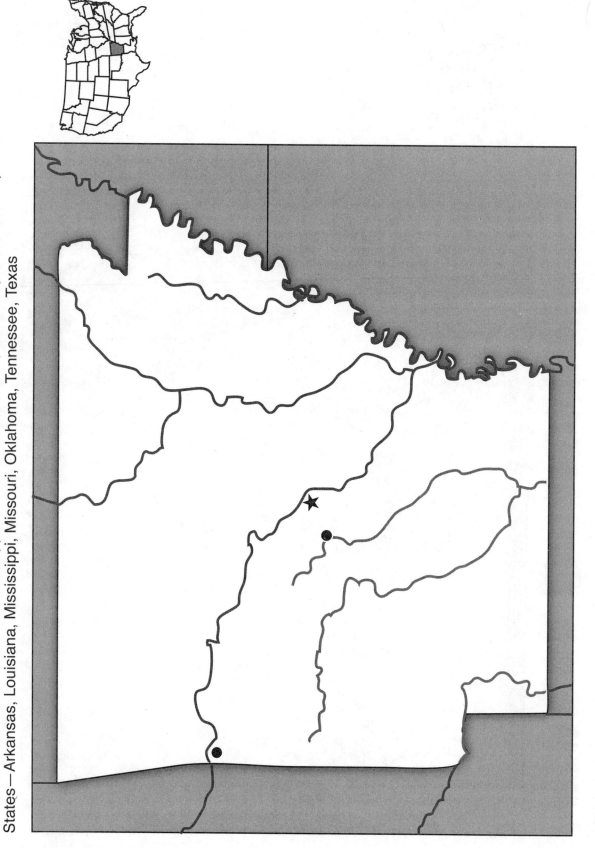

Name: _____

Date: _____

California

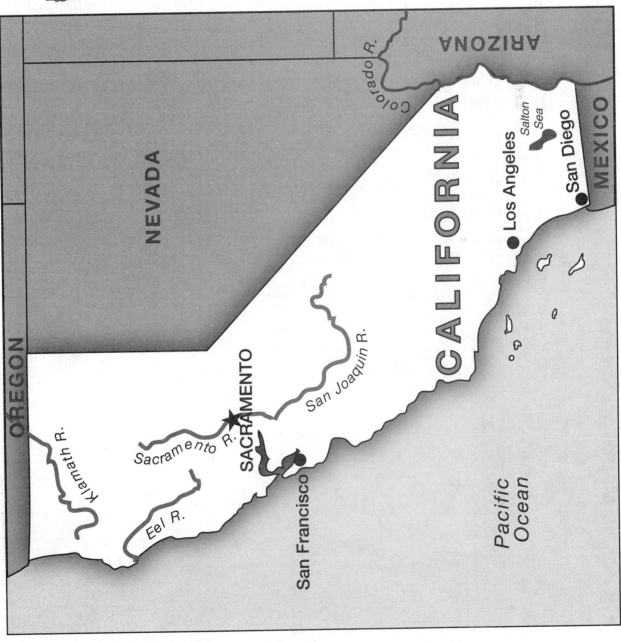

OREGON

NEVADA

ARIZONA

MEXICO

CALIFORNIA

Klamath R.

Eel R.

Sacramento R.

SACRAMENTO

San Joaquin R.

Colorado R.

San Francisco

Los Angeles

Salton Sea

San Diego

Pacific Ocean

Name: _____

Date: _____

California Map Worksheet

Directions: Label the map with the following:

Cities—Los Angeles, Sacramento, San Diego, San Francisco

Rivers—Colorado R., Eel R., Klamath R., Sacramento R., San Joaquin R.

States—Arizona, California, Nevada, Oregon

Bodies of Water—Pacific Ocean, Salton Sea

Country—Mexico

Name: _____

Date: _____

Colorado

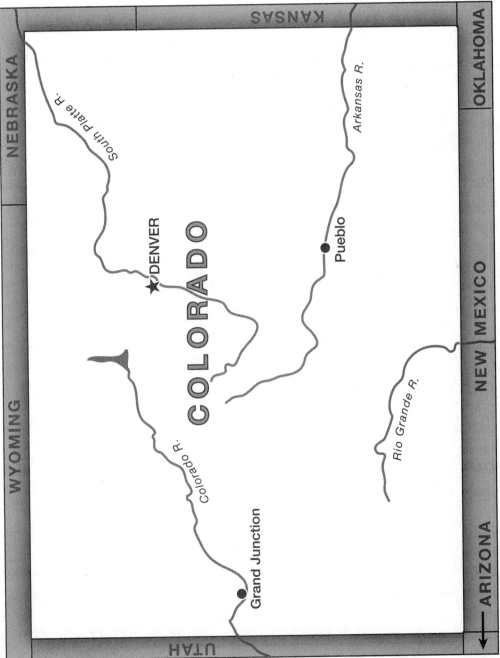

Name: _____   Date: _____

Colorado Map Worksheet

Directions: Label the map with the following:

Cities—Denver, Grand Junction, Pueblo

Rivers—Arkansas R., Colorado R., Rio Grande R., South Platte R.

States—Arizona, Colorado, Kansas, Nebraska, New Mexico, Oklahoma, Utah, Wyoming

Name: _____

Date: _____

Connecticut

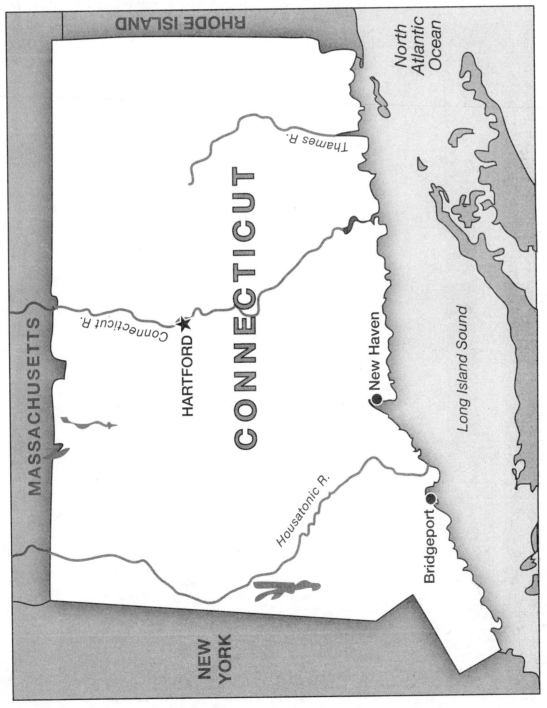

RHODE ISLAND

North Atlantic Ocean

Thames R.

CONNECTICUT

MASSACHUSETTS

Connecticut R.

HARTFORD

Housatonic R.

New Haven

Long Island Sound

Bridgeport

NEW YORK

Name: _____

Date: _____

Connecticut Map Worksheet

Directions: Label the map with the following:

Cities—Bridgeport, Hartford, New Haven

Rivers—Connecticut R., Housatonic R., Thames R.   Bodies of Water—Long Island Sound, North Atlantic Ocean

States—Connecticut, Massachusetts, New York, Rhode Island

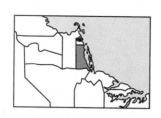

Name: _____

Date: _____

Delaware

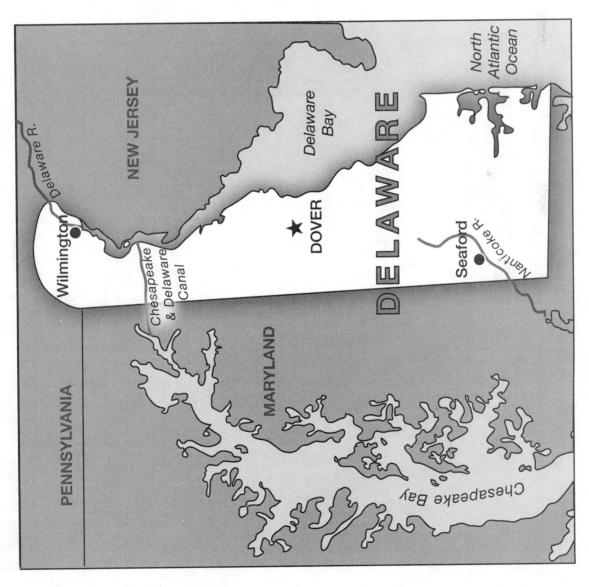

Name: _____

Date: _____

Delaware Map Worksheet

Directions: Label the map with the following:

Cities—Dover, Seaford, Wilmington

Rivers—Delaware R., Nanticoke R.   Bodies of Water—Chesapeake & Delaware Canal, Chesapeake Bay, Delaware Bay,

North Atlantic Ocean   States—Delaware, Maryland, New Jersey, Pennsylvania

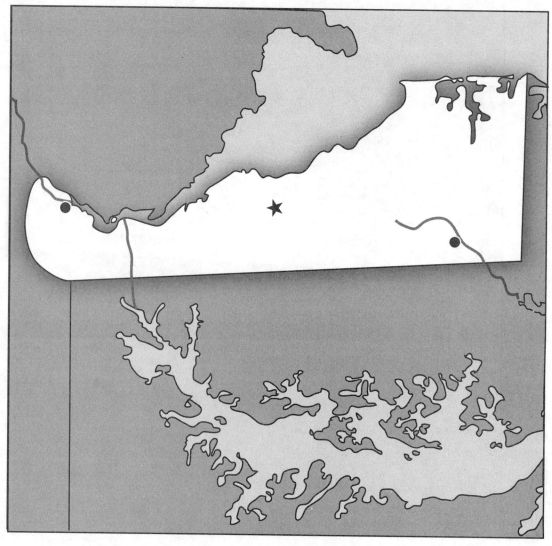

Name: _____

Date: _____

Florida

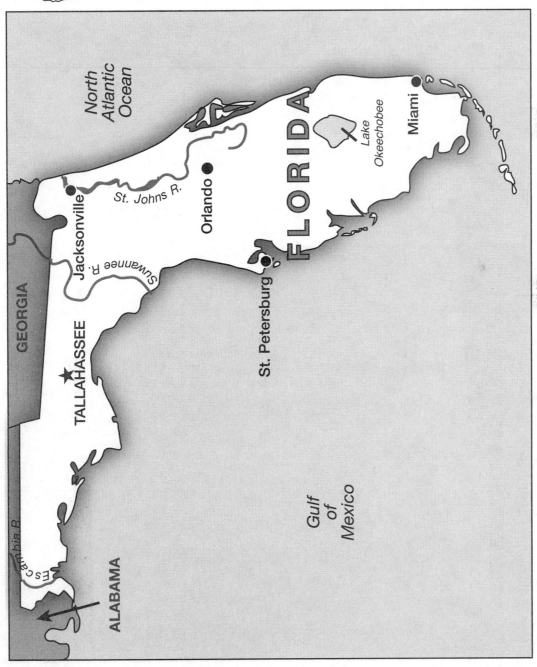

Name: _____

Date: _____

Florida Map Worksheet

Directions: Label the map with the following:

Cities—Jacksonville, Miami, Orlando, St. Petersburg, Tallahassee

Rivers—Escambia R., St. Johns R., Suwannee R.   Bodies of Water—Gulf of Mexico, Lake Okeechobee, North Atlantic Ocean

States—Alabama, Florida, Georgia

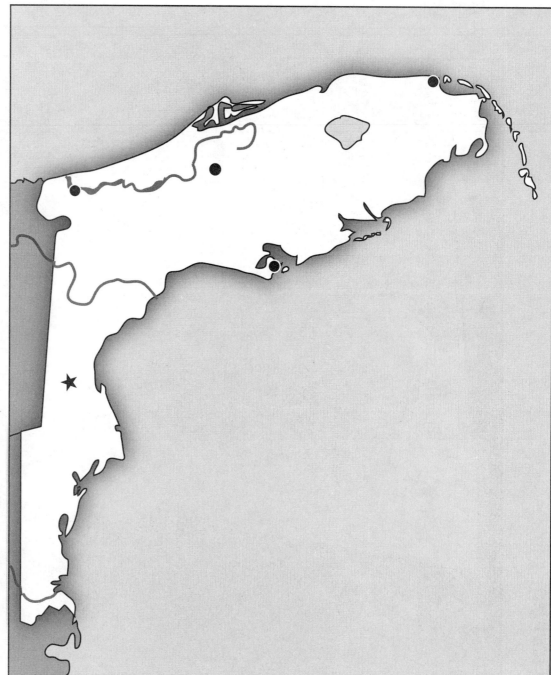

Name: _____

Date: _____

Georgia

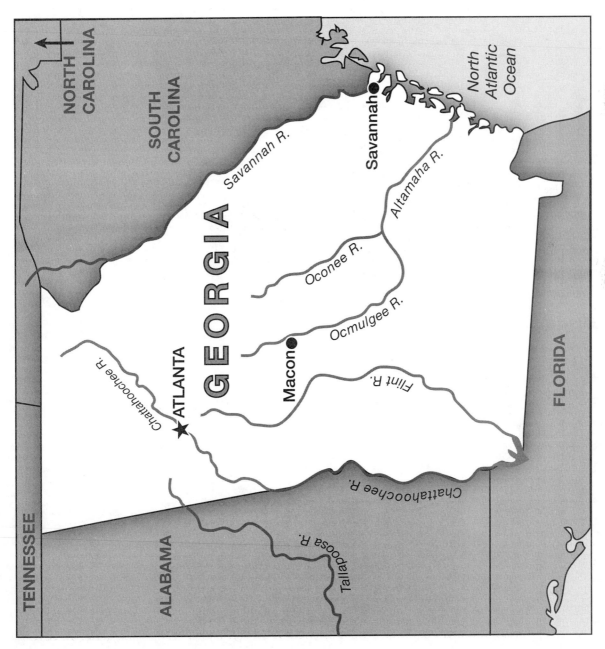

Name: _____

Date: _____

Georgia Map Worksheet

Directions: Label the map with the following:

Cities—Atlanta, Macon, Savannah   Body of Water—North Atlantic Ocean

Rivers—Altamaha R., Chattahoochee R., Flint R., Ocmulgee R., Oconee R., Savannah R.

States—Alabama, Florida, Georgia, North Carolina, South Carolina, Tennessee

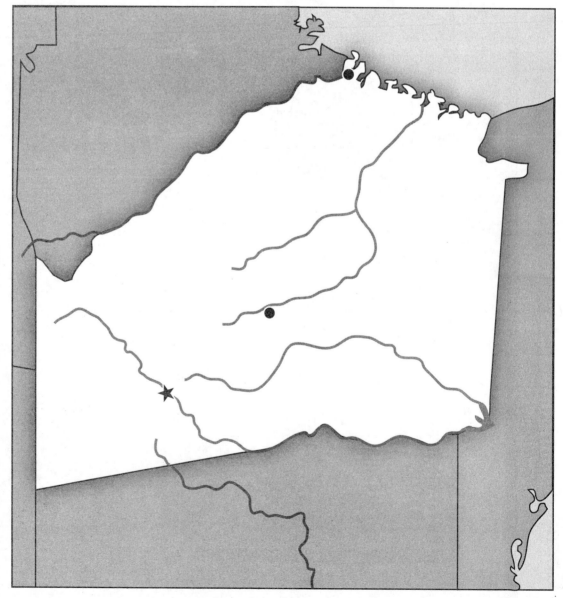

Name: _____

Date: _____

Hawaii

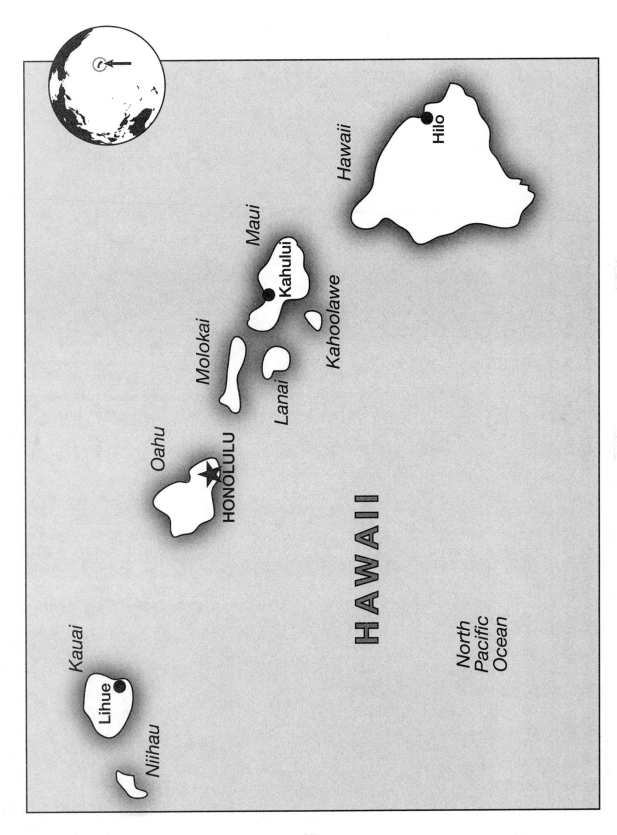

Hilo

Hawaii

Maui

Kahului

Kahoolawe

Molokai

Lanai

Oahu

HONOLULU

HAWAII

Kauai

North
Pacific
Ocean

Lihue

Niihau

Name: _____

Date: _____

Hawaii Map Worksheet

Directions: Label the map with the following:

Cities—Hilo, Honolulu, Kahului, Lihue   Body of Water—North Pacific Ocean

Islands—Hawaii, Kahoolawe, Kauai, Lanai, Maui, Molokai, Niihau, Oahu

Name: _____

Date: _____

Idaho

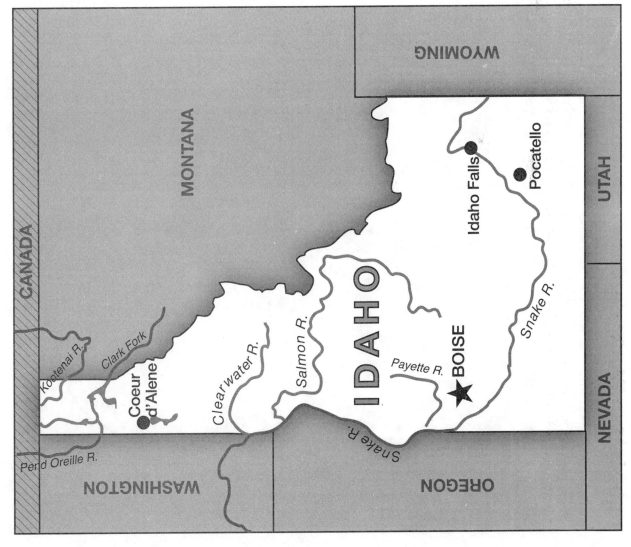

Name: _____

Date: _____

Idaho Map Worksheet

Directions: Label the map with the following:

Cities—Boise, Coeur d'Alene, Idaho Falls, Pocatello

Rivers—Clark Fork, Clearwater R., Kootenai R., Payette R., Pend Oreille R., Salmon R., Snake R.

States—Idaho, Montana, Nevada, Oregon, Utah, Washington, Wyoming   Country—Canada

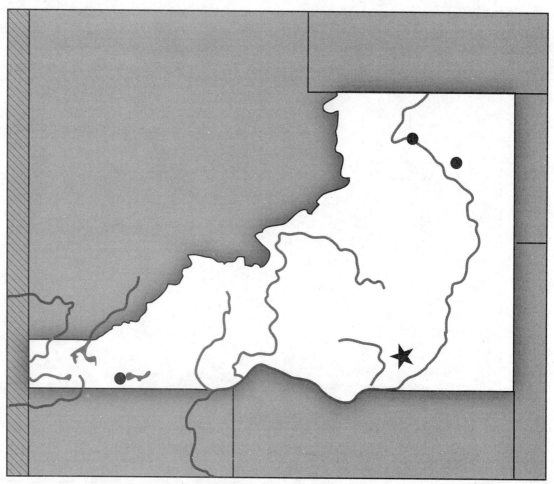

Name:

Date:

Illinois

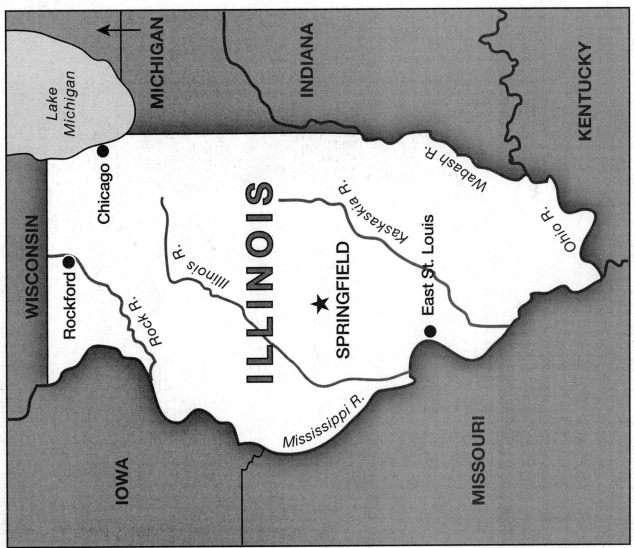

Name: _____

Date: _____

Illinois Map Worksheet

Directions: Label the map with the following:

Cities—Chicago, East St. Louis, Rockford, Springfield

Rivers—Illinois R., Kaskaskia R., Mississippi R., Ohio R., Rock R., Wabash R.

Body of Water—Lake Michigan

States—Illinois, Indiana, Iowa, Kentucky, Michigan, Missouri, Wisconsin

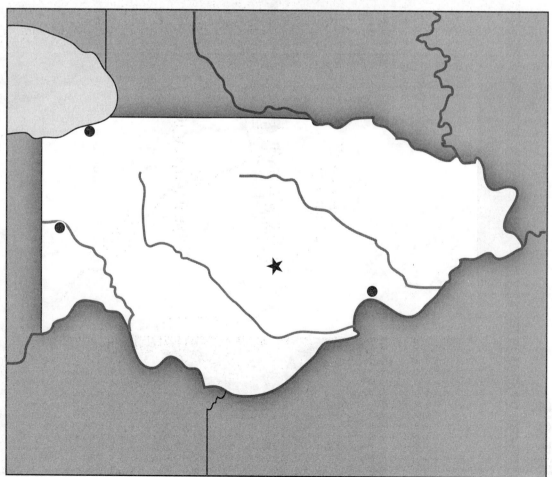

Name: _____

Date: _____

Indiana

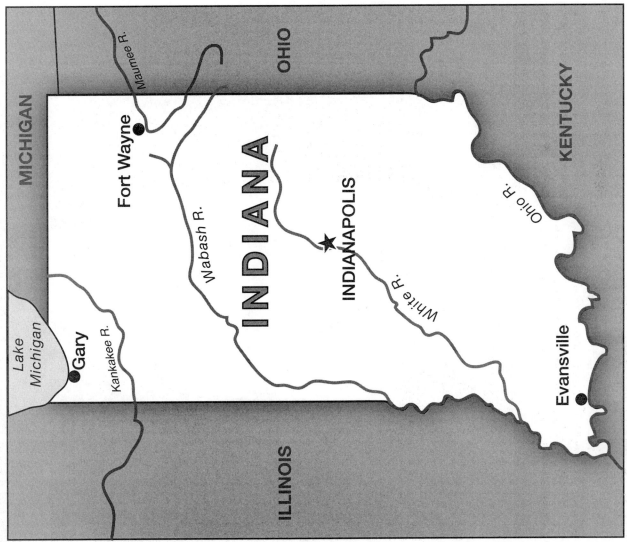

Name: _____

Date: _____

Indiana Map Worksheet

Directions: Label the map with the following:

Cities—Evansville, Fort Wayne, Gary, Indianapolis

Rivers—Kankakee R., Maumee R., Ohio R., Wabash R., White R.

States—Illinois, Indiana, Kentucky, Michigan, Ohio

Body of Water—Lake Michigan

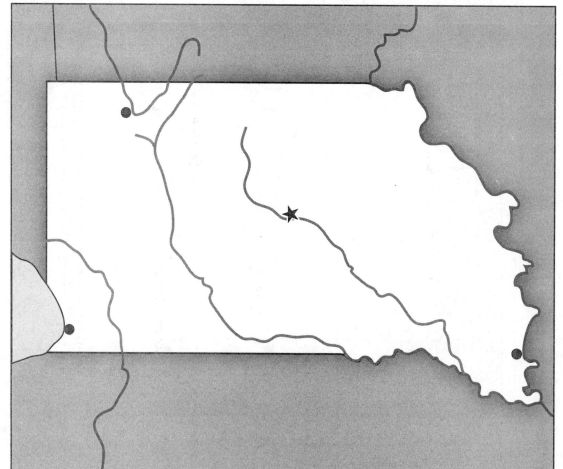

Name: _____

Date: _____

Iowa

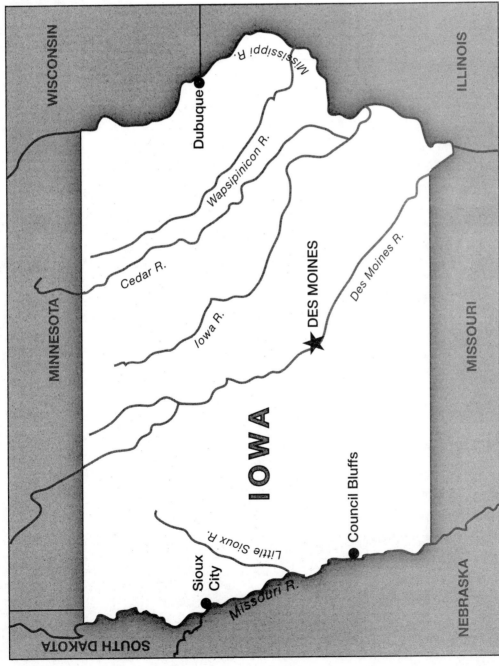

WISCONSIN

MINNESOTA

ILLINOIS

MISSOURI

NEBRASKA

SOUTH DAKOTA

IOWA

Mississippi R.

Dubuque

Wapsipinicon R.

Cedar R.

Iowa R.

DES MOINES

Des Moines R.

Little Sioux R.

Sioux City

Council Bluffs

Missouri R.

Name: _____

Date: _____

Iowa Map Worksheet

Directions: Label the map with the following:

Cities—Council Bluffs, Des Moines, Dubuque, Sioux City

Rivers—Cedar R., Des Moines R., Iowa R., Little Sioux R., Mississippi R., Missouri R., Wapsipinicon R.

States—Illinois, Iowa, Minnesota, Missouri, Nebraska, South Dakota, Wisconsin

Name: _____

Date: _____

Kansas

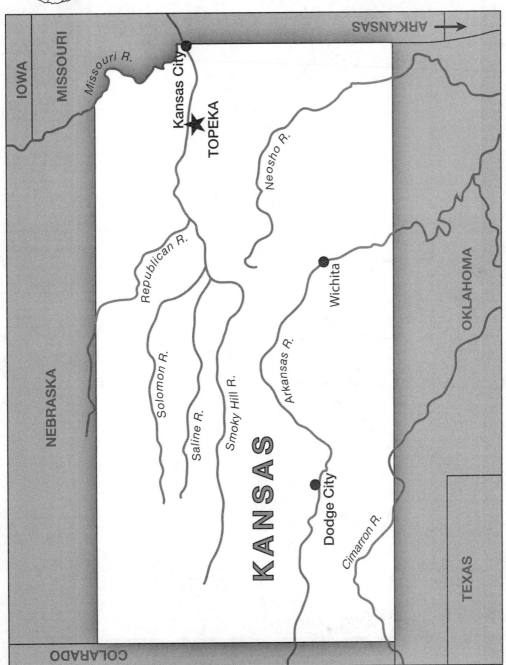

IOWA

MISSOURI

Missouri R.

Kansas City

★ TOPEKA

ARKANSAS →

Neosho R.

Republican R.

Wichita

OKLAHOMA

NEBRASKA

Solomon R.

Saline R.

Smoky Hill R.

Arkansas R.

KANSAS

Dodge City

Cimarron R.

COLORADO

TEXAS

Name: _____

Date: _____

Kansas Map Worksheet

Directions: Label the map with the following:

Cities—Dodge City, Kansas City, Topeka, Wichita

Rivers—Arkansas R., Cimarron R., Missouri R., Neosho R., Republican R., Saline R., Smoky Hill R., Solomon R.

States—Arkansas, Colorado, Iowa, Kansas, Missouri, Nebraska, Oklahoma, Texas

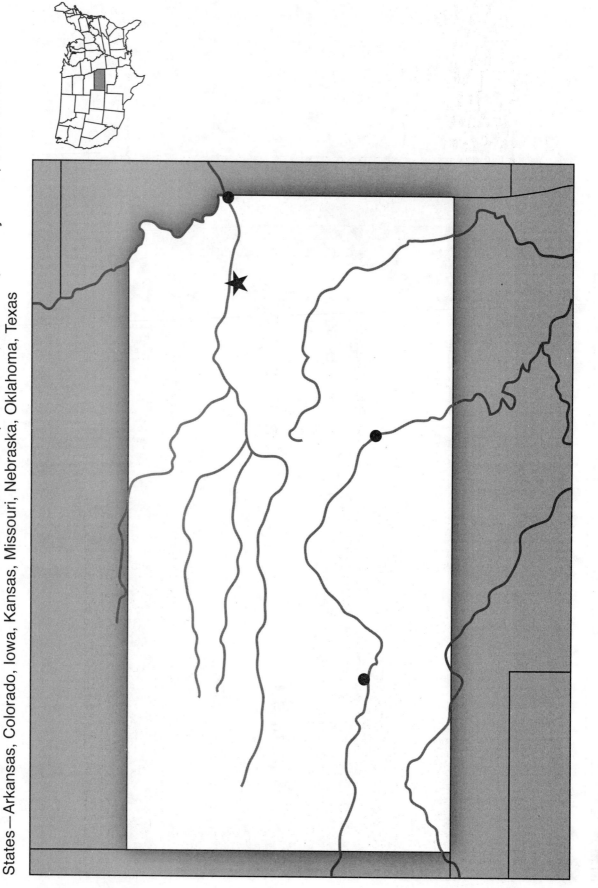

Name: _____

Date: _____

Kentucky

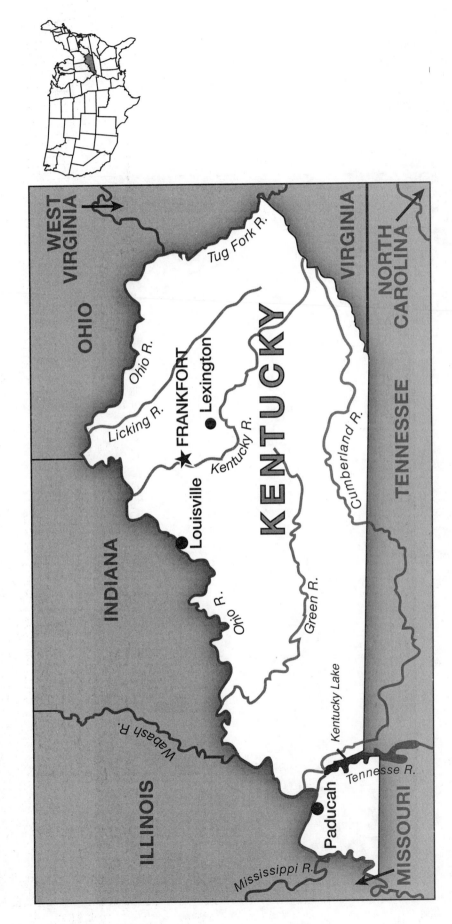

Name: _____

Date: _____

Kentucky Map Worksheet

Directions: Label the map with the following:

Cities—Frankfort, Lexington, Louisville, Paducah

Rivers—Cumberland R., Green R., Kentucky R., Licking R., Mississippi R., Ohio R., Tennessee R., Tug Fork R., Wabash R.

Body of Water—Kentucky Lake

States—Illinois, Indiana, Kentucky, Missouri, North Carolina, Ohio, Tennessee, Virginia, West Virginia

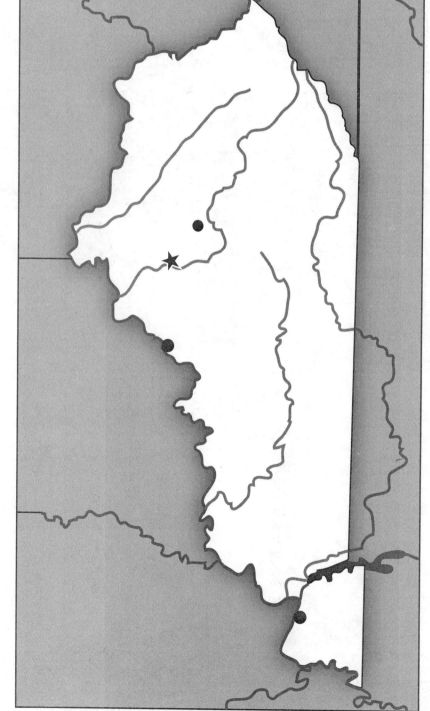

Name: _____

Date: _____

Louisiana

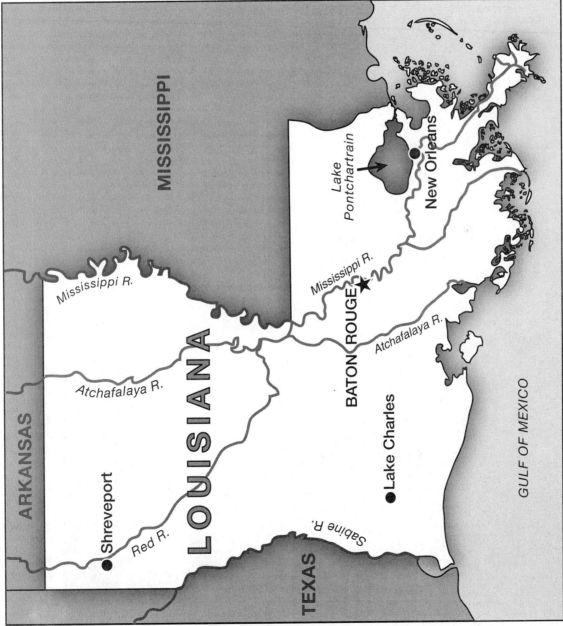

ARKANSAS

MISSISSIPPI

TEXAS

LOUISIANA

Shreveport

Red R.

Sabine R.

Atchafalaya R.

Mississippi R.

Lake Charles

BATON ROUGE ★

Atchafalaya R.

Mississippi R.

Lake Pontchartrain

New Orleans

GULF OF MEXICO

Name: _____

Date: _____

Louisiana Map Worksheet

Directions: Label the map with the following:

Cities—Baton Rouge, Lake Charles, New Orleans, Shreveport

Rivers—Atchafalaya R., Mississippi R., Red R., Sabine R.   Bodies of Water— Gulf of Mexico, Lake Pontchartrain

States—Arkansas, Louisiana, Mississippi, Texas

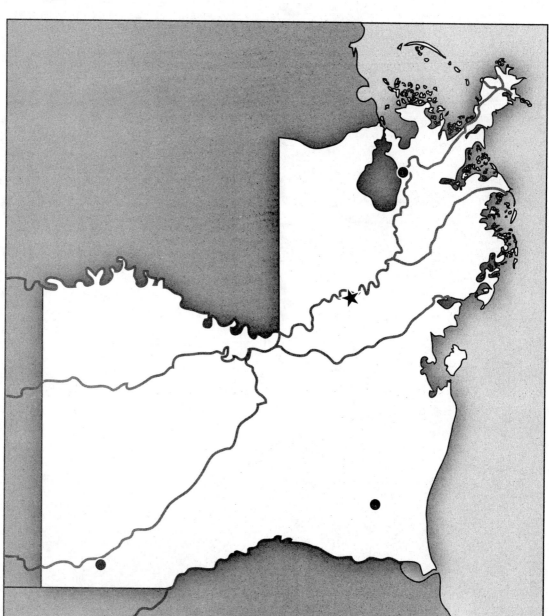

Name:

Maine

Date:

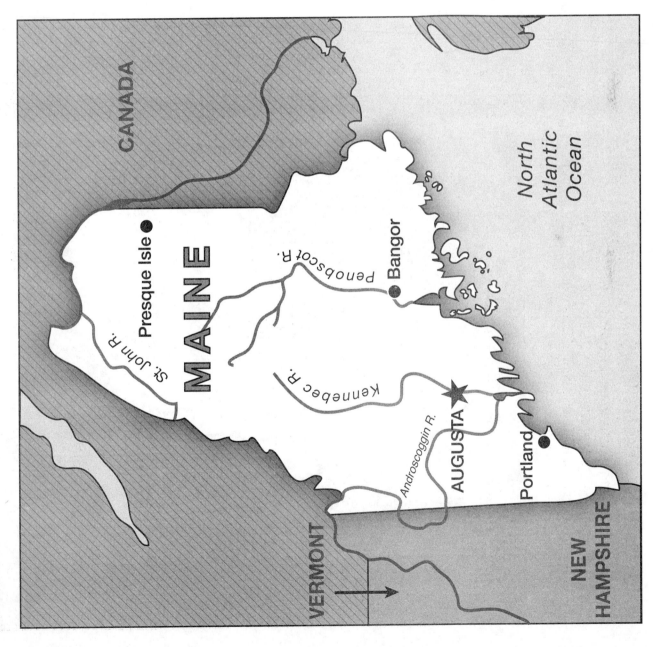

Name: _____

Date: _____

Maine Map Worksheet

Directions: Label the map with the following:

Cities—Augusta, Bangor, Presque Isle, Portland

Rivers—Androscoggin R., Kennebec R., Penobscot R., St. John R.   Body of Water—North Atlantic Ocean

States—Maine, New Hampshire, Vermont   Country—Canada

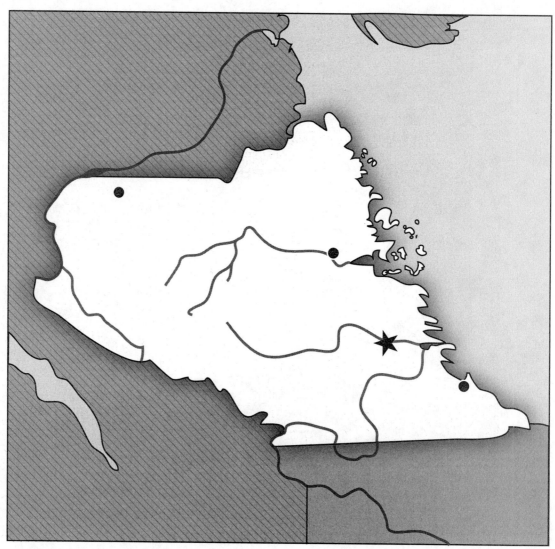

Name: _____

Date: _____

Maryland

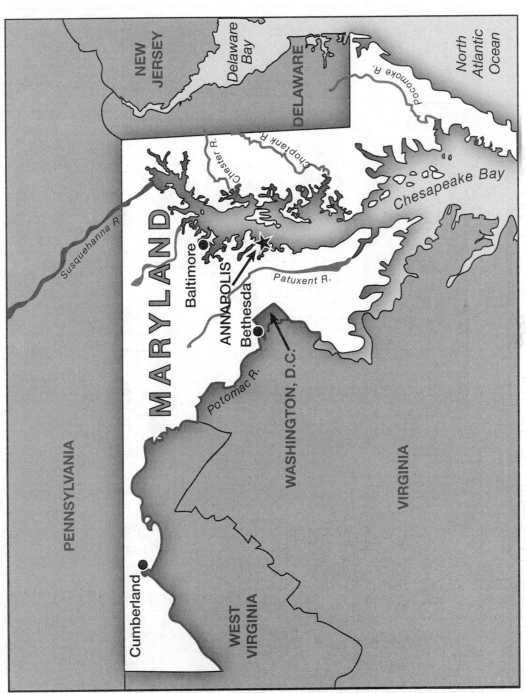

NEW JERSEY

Delaware Bay

DELAWARE

Pocomoke R.

North Atlantic Ocean

Chester R.

Choptank R.

Chesapeake Bay

MARYLAND

Susquehanna R.

Baltimore

ANNAPOLIS

Bethesda

Patuxent R.

WASHINGTON, D.C.

Potomac R.

PENNSYLVANIA

Cumberland

WEST VIRGINIA

VIRGINIA

Name: _____

Date: _____

Maryland Map Worksheet

Directions: Label the map with the following:

Cities—Annapolis, Baltimore, Bethesda, Cumberland, Washington, D.C.

Rivers—Chester R., Choptank R., Patuxent R., Pocomoke R., Potomac R., Susquehanna R.

Bodies of Water—Chesapeake Bay, Delaware Bay, North Atlantic Ocean

States—Delaware, Maryland, New Jersey, Pennsylvania, Virginia, West Virginia

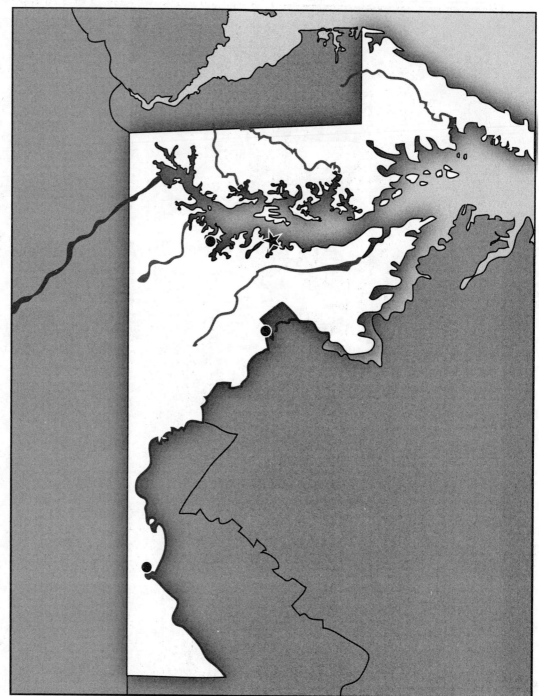

Name: _____

Date: _____

Massachusetts

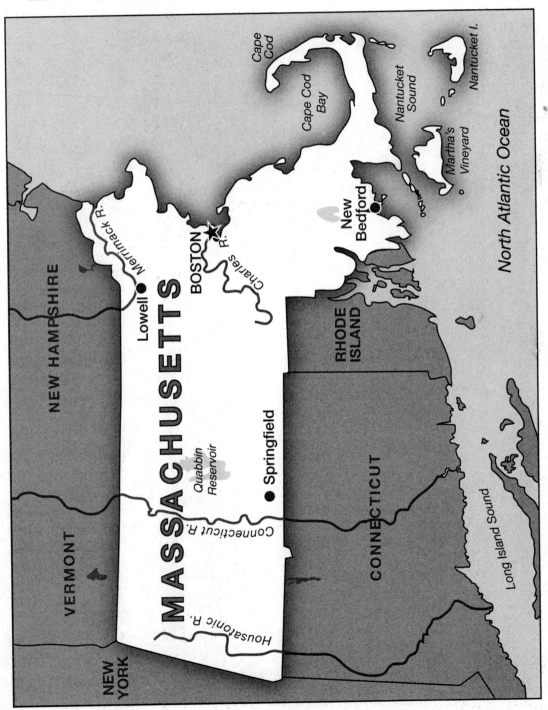

NEW HAMPSHIRE

VERMONT

NEW YORK

MASSACHUSETTS

Lowell

BOSTON

Merrimack R.

Charles R.

Quabbin Reservoir

Springfield

Connecticut R.

Housatonic R.

New Bedford

RHODE ISLAND

CONNECTICUT

Cape Cod

Cape Cod Bay

Nantucket Sound

Nantucket I.

Martha's Vineyard

North Atlantic Ocean

Long Island Sound

Name: _____

Date: _____

Massachusetts Map Worksheet

Directions: Label the map with the following:

Cities—Boston, Lowell, New Bedford, Springfield   Landforms— Cape Cod, Martha's Vineyard, Nantucket Island
Rivers—Charles R., Connecticut R., Housatonic R., Merrimack R.
Bodies of Water—Cape Cod Bay, Long Island Sound, Nantucket Sound, North Atlantic Ocean, Quabbin Reservoir
States—Connecticut, Massachusetts, New Hampshire, New York, Rhode Island, Vermont

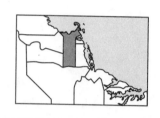

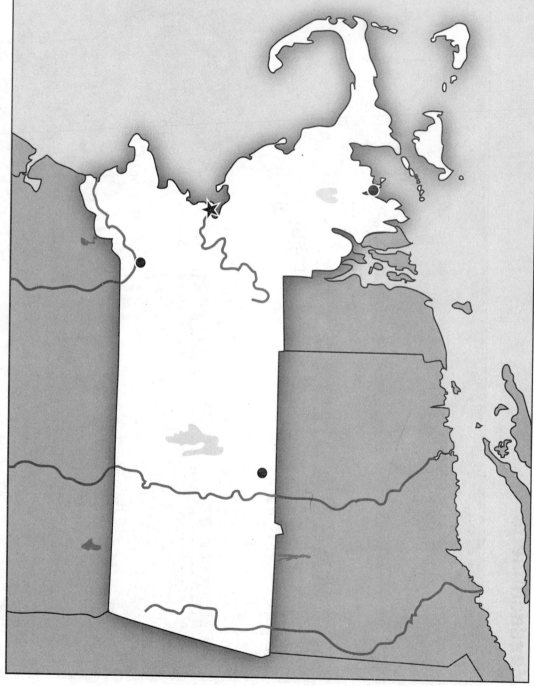

Name:

Date:

Michigan

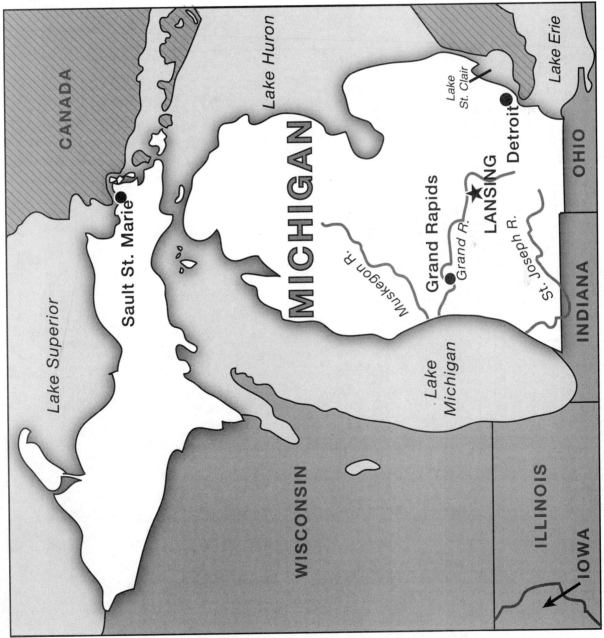

CANADA

Lake Superior

Lake Huron

Sault St. Marie

MICHIGAN

Grand Rapids

Muskegon R.

Grand R.

LANSING

Lake St. Clair

Detroit

Lake Erie

St. Joseph R.

Lake Michigan

OHIO

INDIANA

WISCONSIN

ILLINOIS

IOWA

Name: _____

Date: _____

Michigan Map Worksheet

Directions: Label the map with the following:

Cities—Detroit, Grand Rapids, Lansing, Sault St. Marie   Rivers—Grand R., Muskegon R., St. Joseph R.

Bodies of Water—Lake Erie, Lake Huron, Lake Michigan, Lake St. Clair, Lake Superior

States—Illinois, Indiana, Iowa, Michigan, Wisconsin   Country—Canada

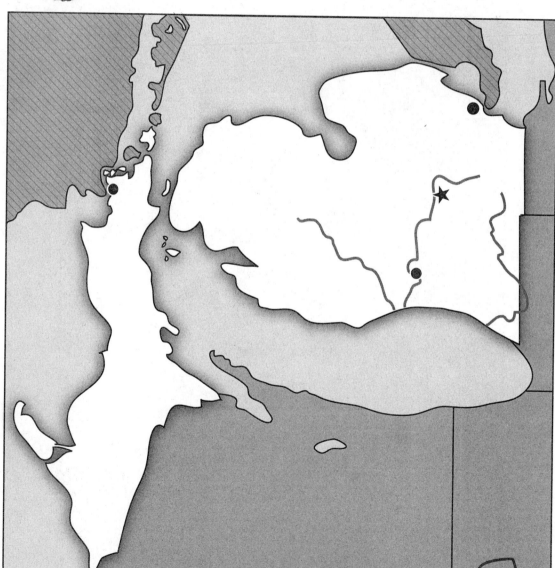

Name: _____

Date: _____

Minnesota

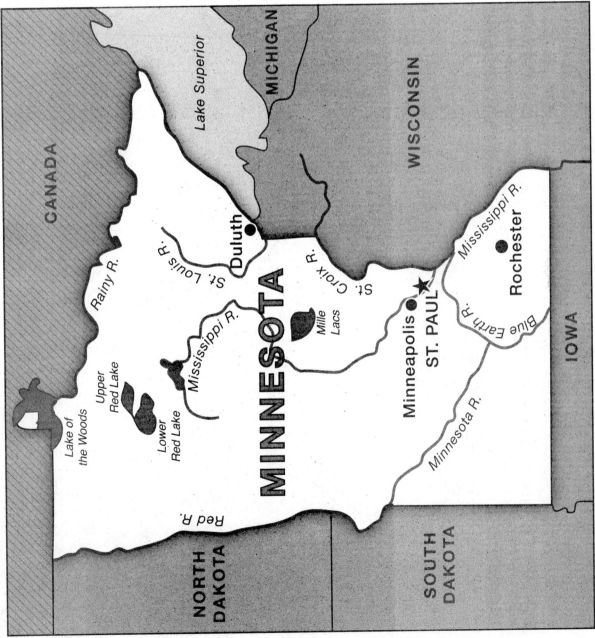

Name: _____

Date: _____

Minnesota Map Worksheet

Directions: Label the map with the following:

Cities—Duluth, Minneapolis, Rochester, St. Paul

Bodies of Water—Lake of the Woods, Lake Superior, Lower Red Lake, Mille Lacs, Upper Red Lake

Rivers—Blue Earth R., Minnesota R., Mississippi R., Rainy R., Red R., St. Croix R., St. Louis R.

States—Iowa, Michigan, Minnesota, North Dakota, South Dakota, Wisconsin   Country—Canada

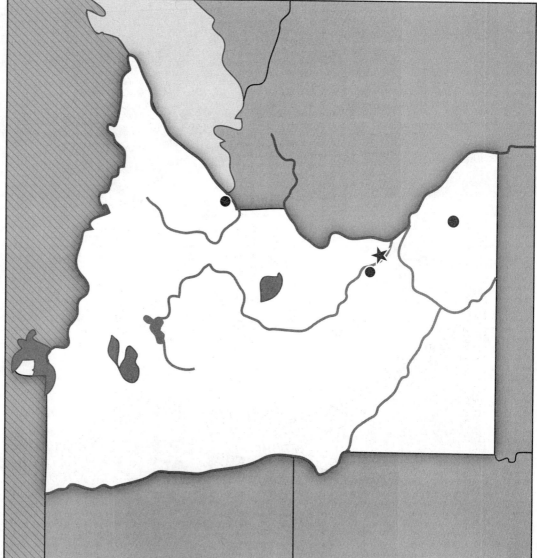

Name: _____

Date: _____

Mississippi

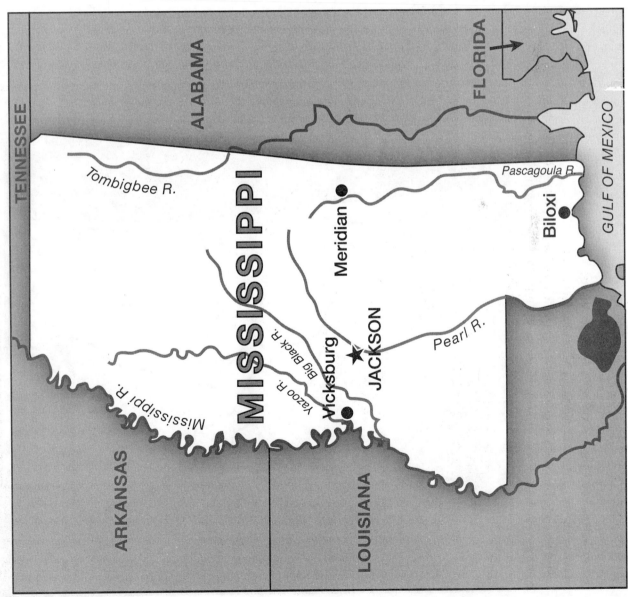

TENNESSEE

ALABAMA

FLORIDA

GULF OF MEXICO

Tombigbee R.

Pascagoula R.

MISSISSIPPI

Meridian

Biloxi

Mississippi R.

Yazoo R.

Big Black R.

Vicksburg

JACKSON

Pearl R.

ARKANSAS

LOUISIANA

Name: _____

Date: _____

Mississippi Map Worksheet

Directions: Label the map with the following:

Cities—Biloxi, Jackson, Meridian, Vicksburg

Rivers—Big Black R., Mississippi R., Pascagoula R., Pearl R., Tombigbee R., Yazoo R.,

States—Alabama, Arkansas, Florida, Lousiana, Mississippi, Tennessee

Body of Water—Gulf of Mexico

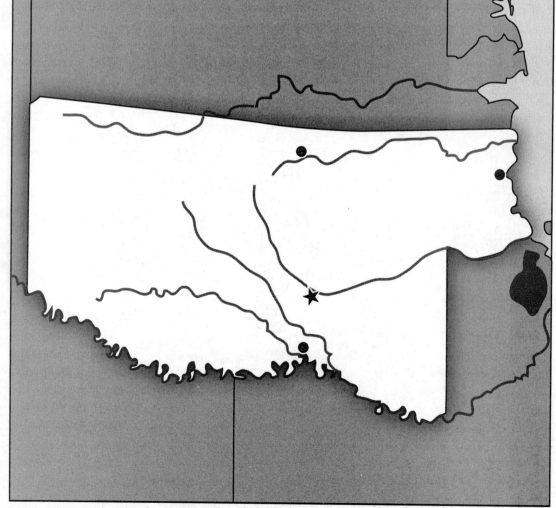

Name:

Date:

Missouri

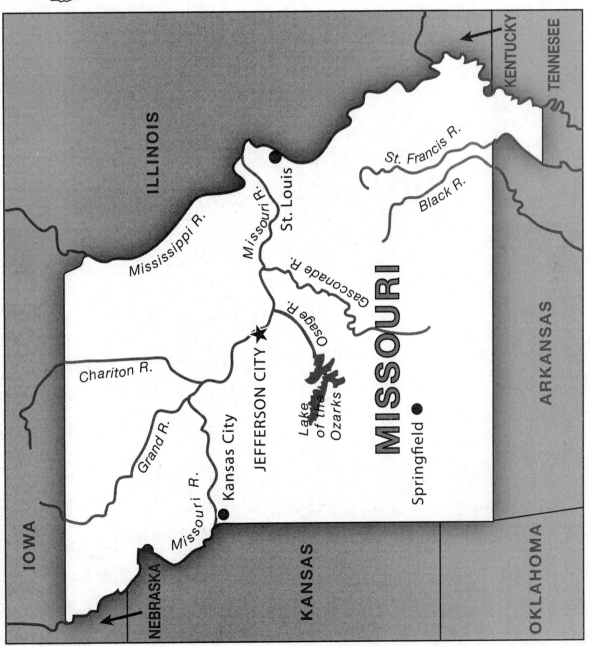

TENNESSEE

KENTUCKY

ILLINOIS

St. Francis R.

Black R.

Missouri R.

St. Louis

Mississippi R.

Gasconade R.

MISSOURI

Osage R.

ARKANSAS

Chariton R.

JEFFERSON CITY

Lake of the Ozarks

Springfield

Grand R.

Kansas City

Missouri R.

IOWA

NEBRASKA

KANSAS

OKLAHOMA

Name: _____

Date: _____

Missouri Map Worksheet

Directions: Label the map with the following:

Cities—Jefferson City, Kansas City, Springfield, St. Louis   Body of Water—Lake of the Ozarks

Rivers—Black R., Chariton R., Gasconade R., Grand R., Mississippi R., Missouri R., Osage R., St. Francis R.

States—Arkansas, Illinois, Iowa, Kansas, Kentucky, Missouri, Nebraska, Oklahoma, Tennessee

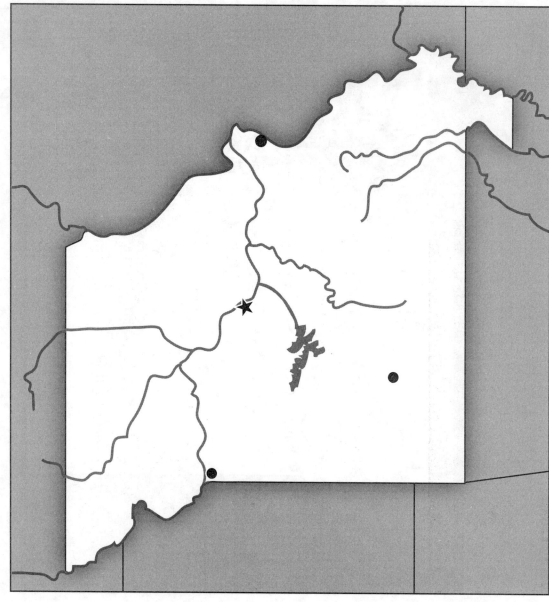

Montana

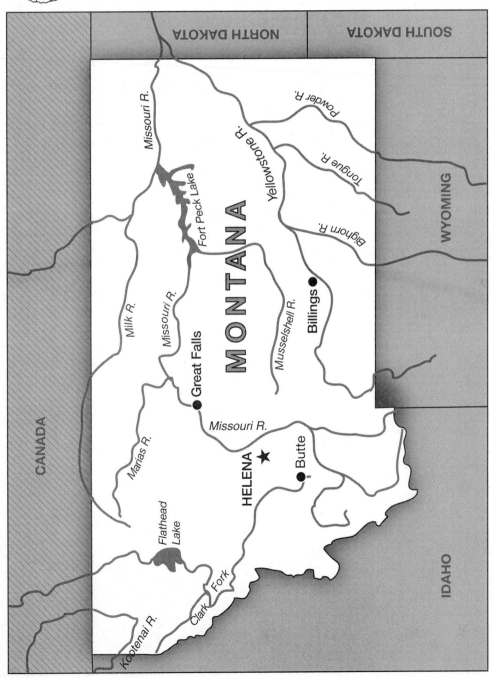

Name: _____

Date: _____

Montana Map Worksheet

Directions: Label the map with the following:

Cities—Billings, Butte, Great Falls, Helena

Rivers—Bighorn R., Clark Fork, Kootenai R., Marias R., Milk R., Missouri R., Musselshell R., Powder R., Tongue R., Yellowstone R.   Bodies of Water—Flathead Lake, Fort Peck Lake

States—Idaho, Montana, North Dakota, South Dakota, Wyoming   Country—Canada

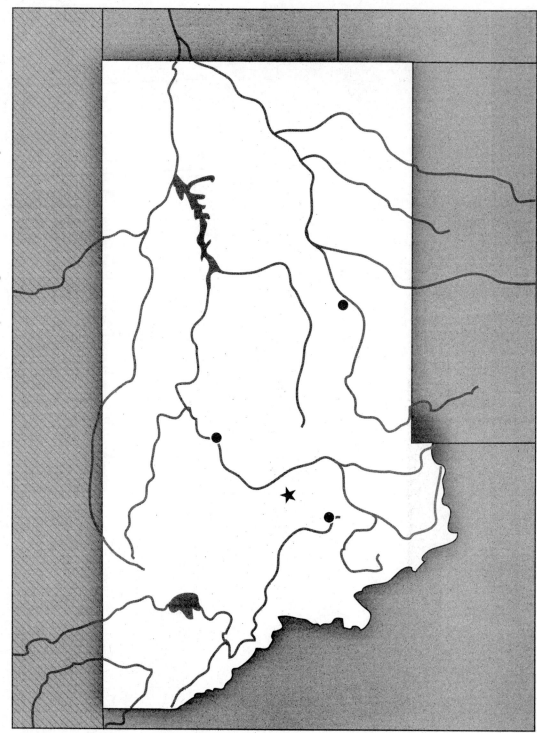

Nebraska

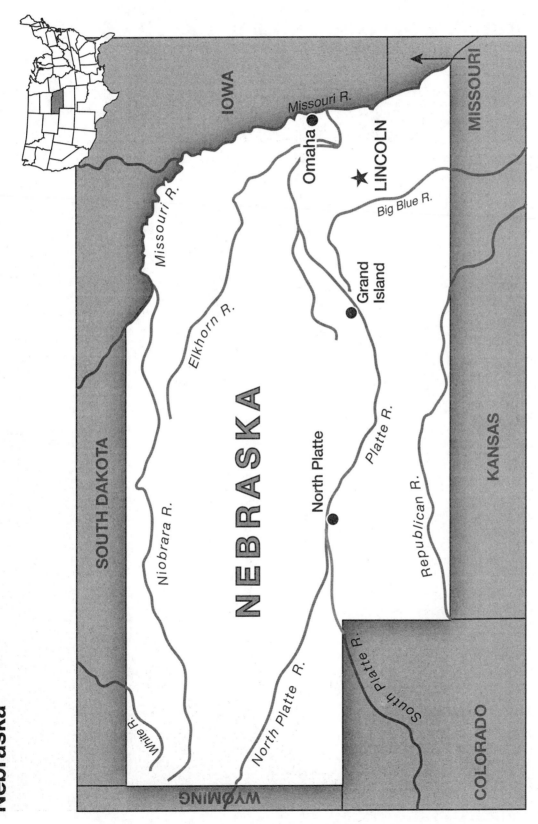

Name: _____

Date: _____

Nebraska Map Worksheet

Directions: Label the map with the following:

Cities—Grand Island, Lincoln, North Platte, Omaha

Rivers—Big Blue R., Elkhorn R., Missouri R., Niobrara R., North Platte R., Platte R., Republican R., South Platte R., White R.

States—Colorado, Iowa, Kansas, Missouri, Nebraska, South Dakota, Wyoming

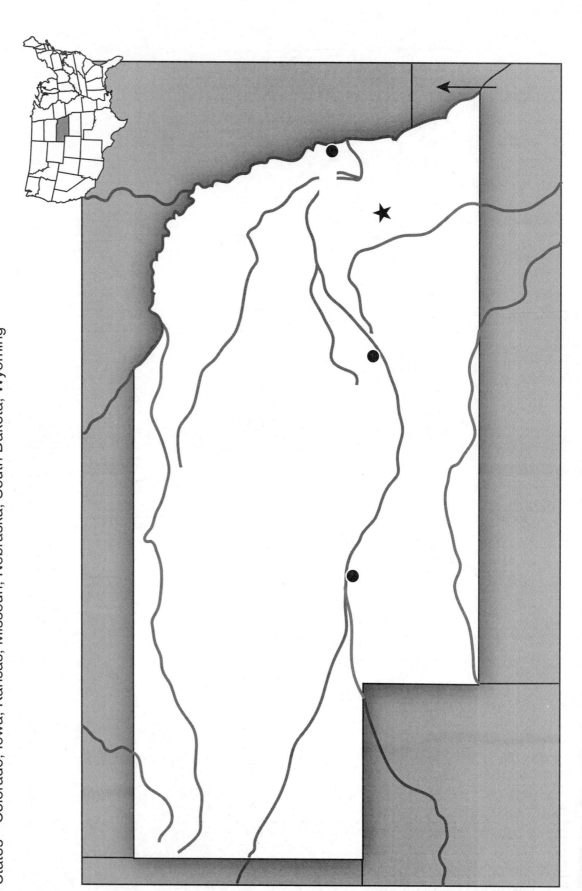

Nevada

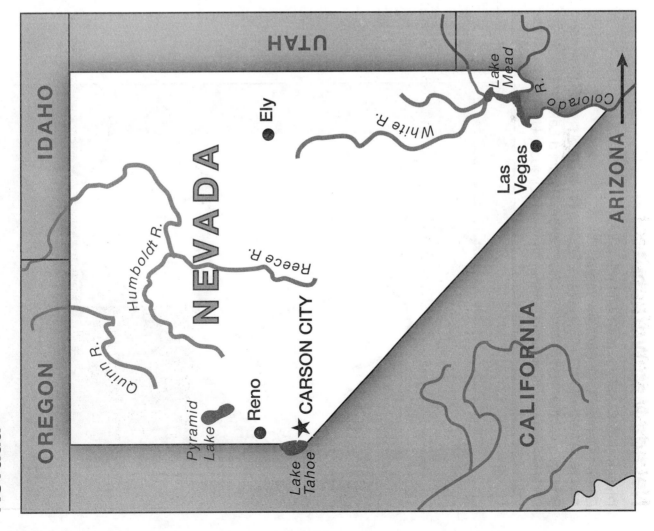

Name: _____

Date: _____

Nevada Map Worksheet

Directions: Label the map with the following:

Cities—Carson City, Ely, Las Vegas, Reno

Rivers—Colorado R., Humboldt R., Quinn R., Reece R., White R.

Bodies of Water—Lake Mead, Lake Tahoe, Pyramid Lake

States—Arizona, California, Idaho, Nevada, Oregon, Utah

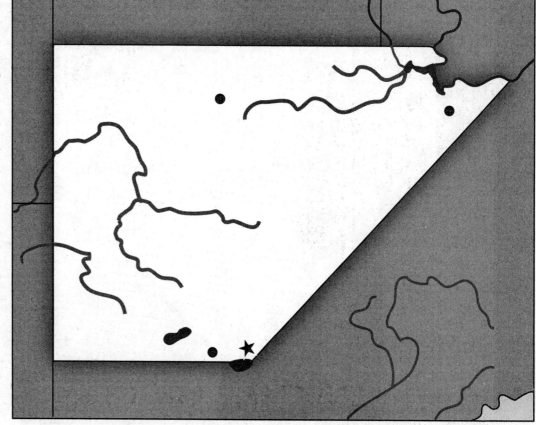

Name: _____

Date: _____

New Hampshire

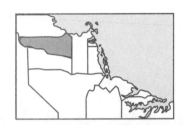

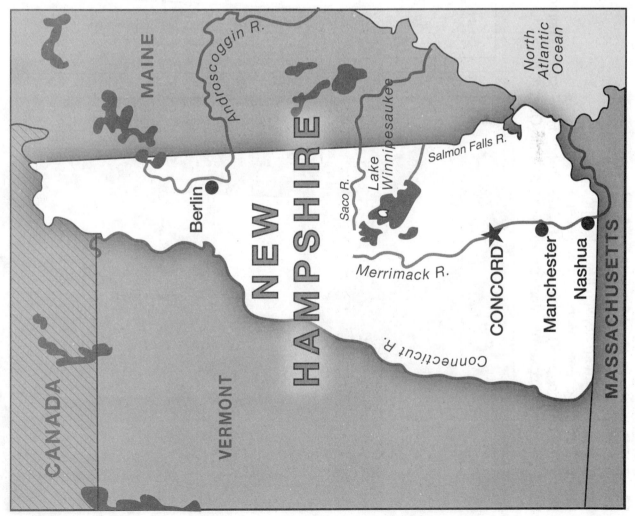

Name: _____

Date: _____

New Hampshire Map Worksheet

Directions: Label the map with the following:

Cities—Berlin, Concord, Manchester, Nashua

Rivers—Androscoggin R., Connecticut R., Merrimack R., Saco R., Salmon Falls R.   Country—Canada

Bodies of Water—Lake Winnipesaukee, North Atlantic Ocean   States—Maine, Massachusetts, New Hampshire, Vermont

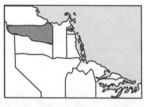

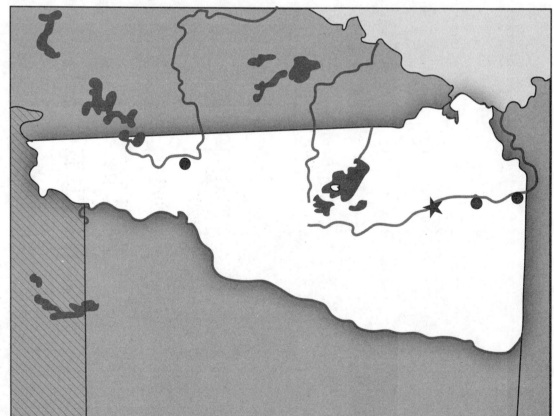

Name: _____

Date: _____

New Jersey

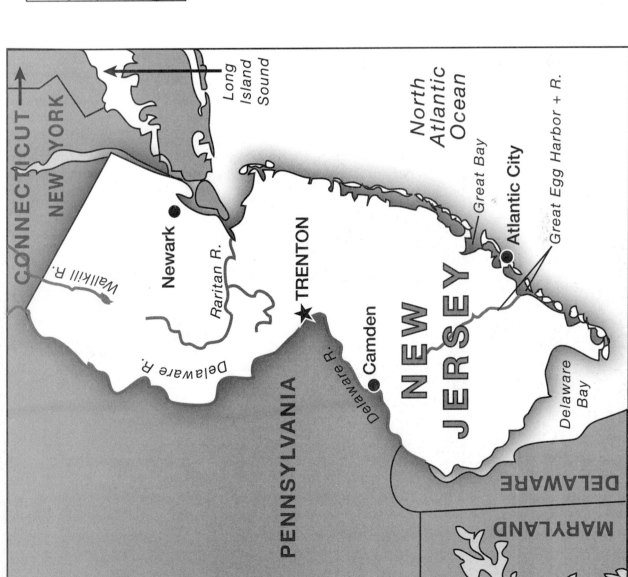

CONNECTICUT

NEW YORK

Long Island Sound

Wallkill R.

Newark

Raritan R.

Delaware R.

TRENTON

PENNSYLVANIA

Delaware R.

Camden

NEW JERSEY

North Atlantic Ocean

Great Bay

Atlantic City

Great Egg Harbor + R.

Delaware Bay

DELAWARE

MARYLAND

Name: _____

Date: _____

New Jersey Map Worksheet

Directions: Label the map with the following:

Cities—Atlantic City, Camden, Newark, Trenton

Rivers—Delaware R., Great Egg R., Raritan R., Wallkill R.

Bodies of Water—Delaware Bay, Great Bay, Great Egg Harbor, Long Island Sound, North Atlantic Ocean

States—Connecticut, Delaware, Maryland, New Jersey, New York, Pennsylvania

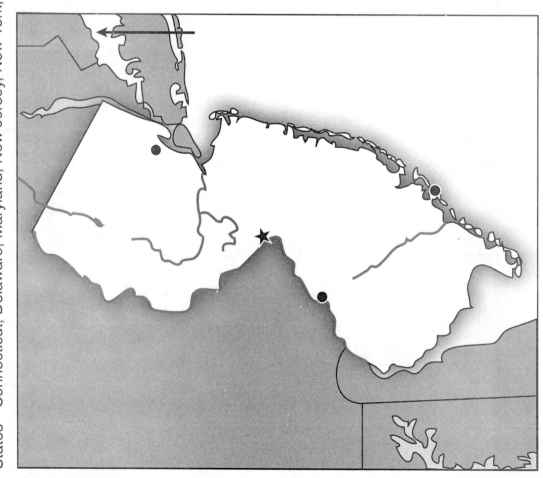

Name: _____

Date: _____

New Mexico

Name: _____ Date: _____

New Mexico Map Worksheet

Directions: Label the map with the following:

Cities—Albuquerque, Carlsbad, Las Cruces, Santa Fe

Rivers—Canadian R., Gila R., Pecos R., Rio Grande R., San Juan R.

States—Arizona, Colorado, New Mexico, Oklahoma, Texas, Utah

Country—Mexico

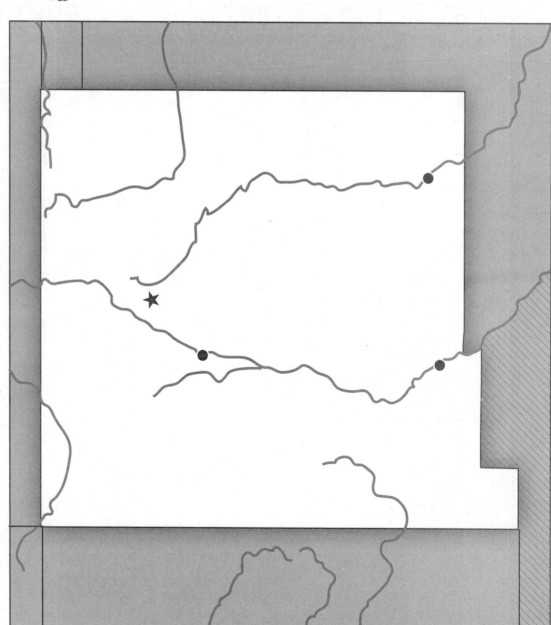

Name: _____

Date: _____

New York

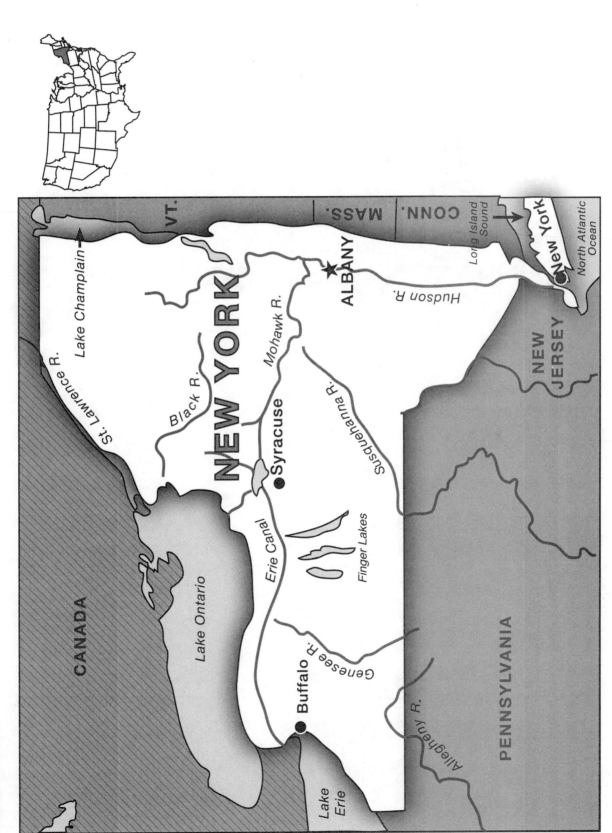

Name: _____

Date: _____

New York Map Worksheet

Directions: Label the map with the following:

Cities—Albany, Buffalo, New York, Syracuse

Rivers—Allegheny R., Black R., Genesee R., Hudson R., Mohawk R., St. Lawrence R., Susquehanna R.

Bodies of Water—Erie Canal, Finger Lakes, Lake Champlain, Lake Erie, Lake Ontario, Long Island Sound, North Atlantic Ocean

States—Connecticut, Massachusetts, New Jersey, New York, Pennsylvania, Vermont   Country—Canada

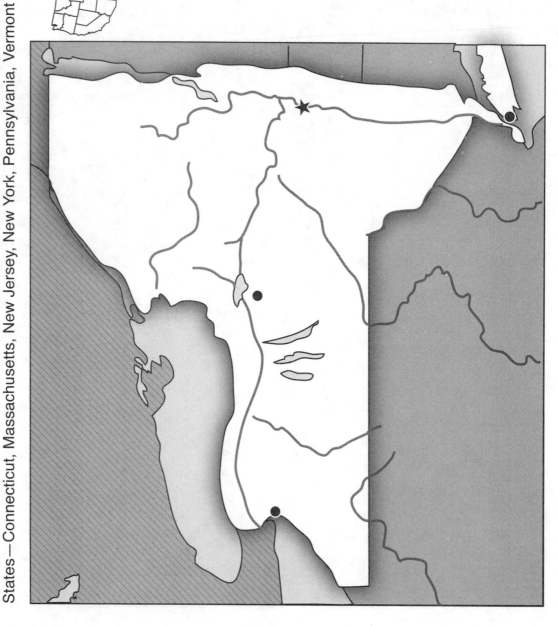

Name: _____

Date: _____

North Carolina

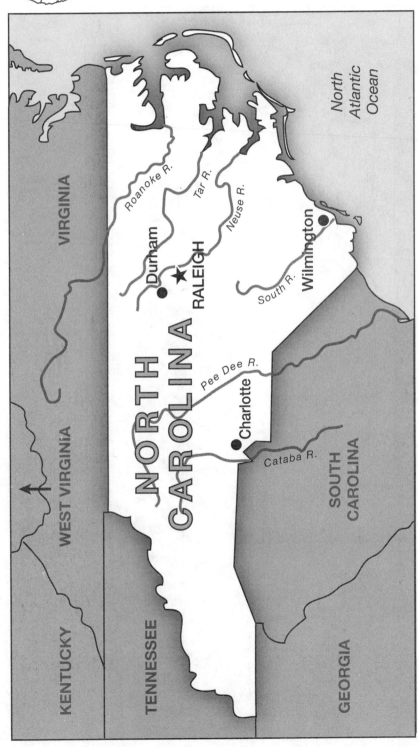

- VIRGINIA
- KENTUCKY
- WEST VIRGINIA
- TENNESSEE
- GEORGIA
- SOUTH CAROLINA
- NORTH CAROLINA
- North Atlantic Ocean
- Roanoke R.
- Tar R.
- Neuse R.
- South R.
- Pee Dee R.
- Cataba R.
- Durham
- RALEIGH ★
- Wilmington
- Charlotte

Name: _____ Date: _____

North Carolina Map Worksheet

Directions: Label the map with the following:

Cities—Charlotte, Durham, Raleigh, Wilmington

Rivers—Cataba R., Neuse R., Pee Dee R., Roanoke R., South R., Tar R.   Body of Water—North Atlantic Ocean

States—Georgia, Kentucky, North Carolina, South Carolina, Tennessee, Virginia, West Virginia

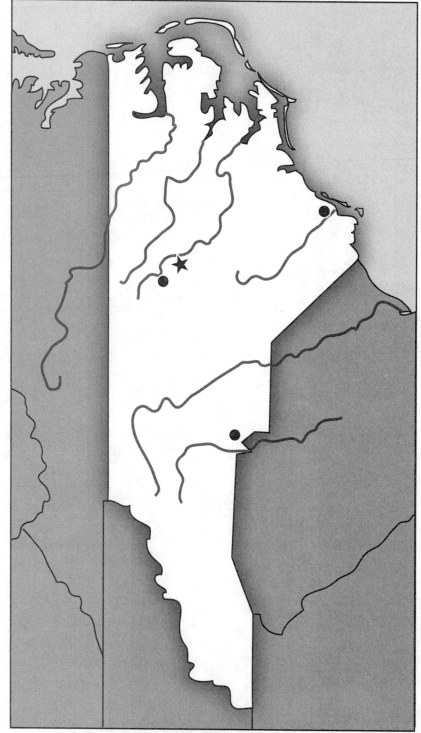

Name: _____

Date: _____

North Dakota

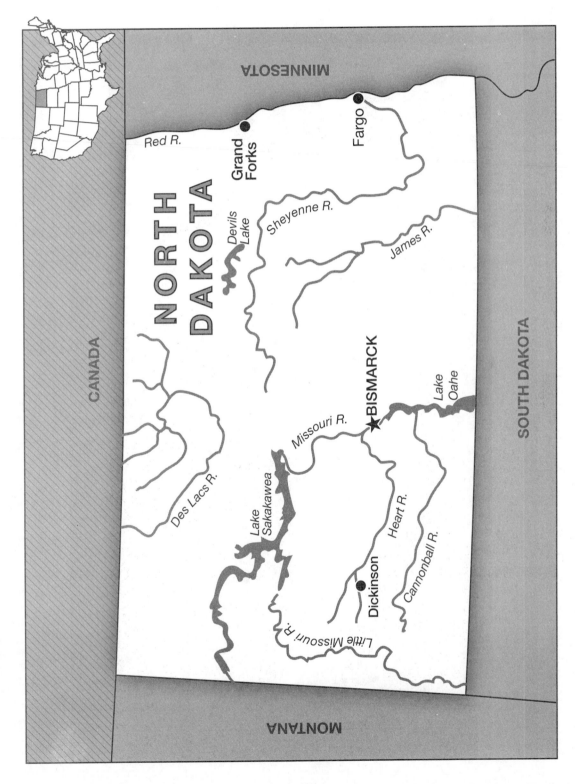

Name: _____ Date: _____

North Dakota Map Worksheet

Directions: Label the map with the following:

Cities—Bismarck, Dickinson, Fargo, Grand Forks

Rivers—Cannonball R., Des Lacs R., Heart R., James R. Little Missouri R., Missouri R., Red R., Sheyenne R.

Bodies of Water—Devils Lake, Lake Oahe, Lake Sakakawea

States—Minnesota, Montana, North Dakota, South Dakota   Country—Canada

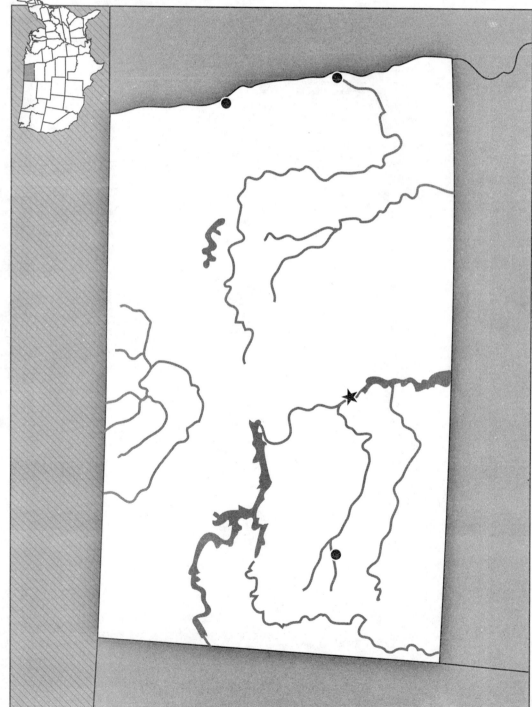

Name: _____

Date: _____

Ohio

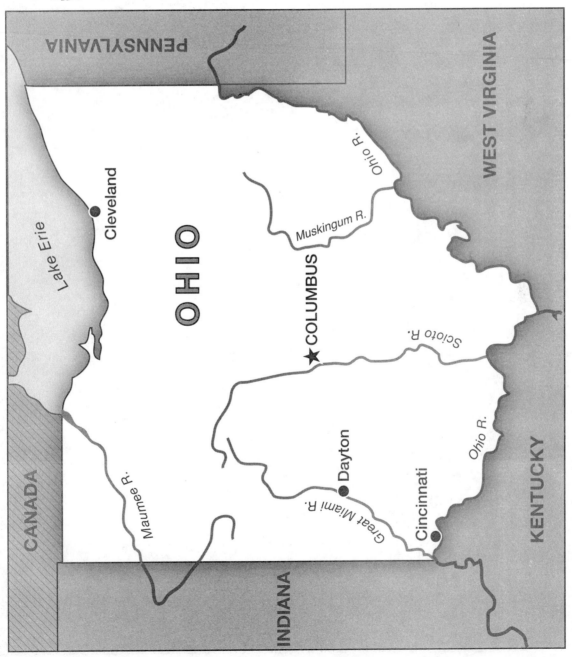

PENNSYLVANIA

WEST VIRGINIA

CANADA

Lake Erie

Cleveland

OHIO

★ COLUMBUS

Muskingum R.

Ohio R.

Scioto R.

Dayton

Great Miami R.

Maumee R.

Cincinnati

Ohio R.

INDIANA

KENTUCKY

Name: _____

Date: _____

Ohio Map Worksheet

Directions: Label the map with the following:

Cities—Cincinnati, Cleveland, Columbus, Dayton

Rivers—Great Miami R., Maumee R., Muskingum R., Ohio R., Scioto R.

Body of Water—Lake Erie

Country—Canada

States—Indiana, Kentucky, Ohio, Pennsylvania, West Virginia

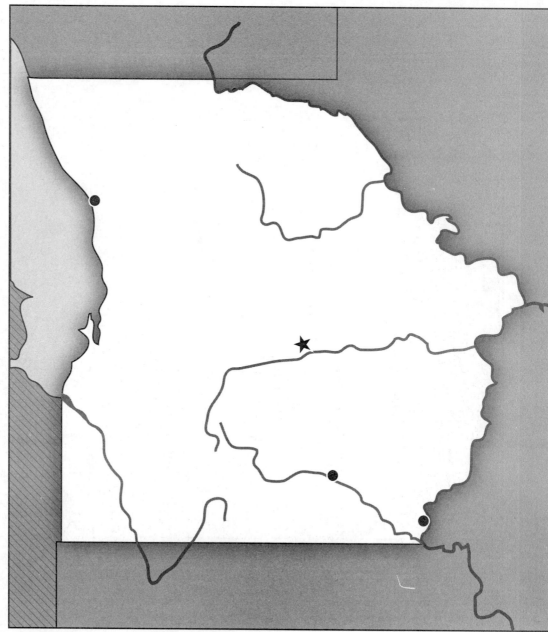

Name: _____

Oklahoma

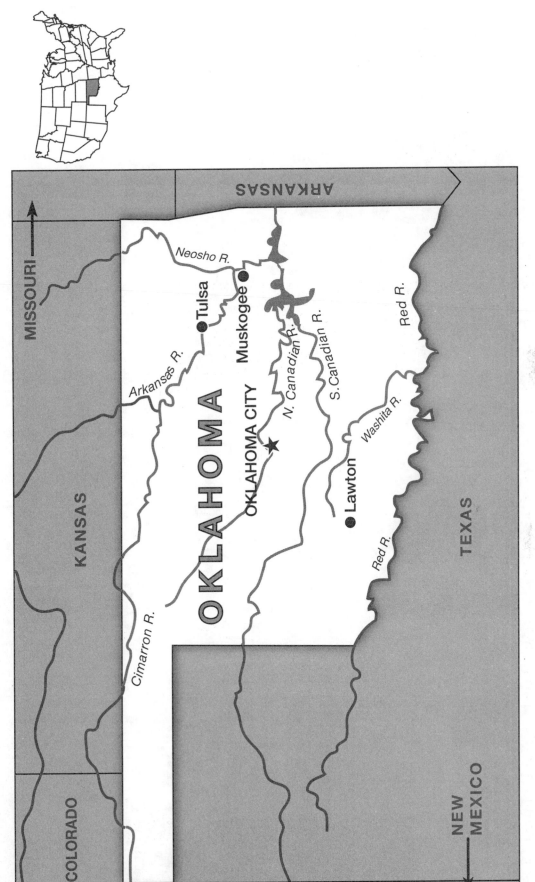

Name: _____

Date: _____

Oklahoma Map Worksheet

Directions: Label the map with the following:

Cities—Lawton, Muskogee, Oklahoma City, Tulsa

Rivers—Arkansas R., Cimarron R., Neosho R., N. Canadian R., Red R., S. Canadian R., Washita R.

States—Arkansas, Colorado, Kansas, Missouri, New Mexico, Oklahoma, Texas

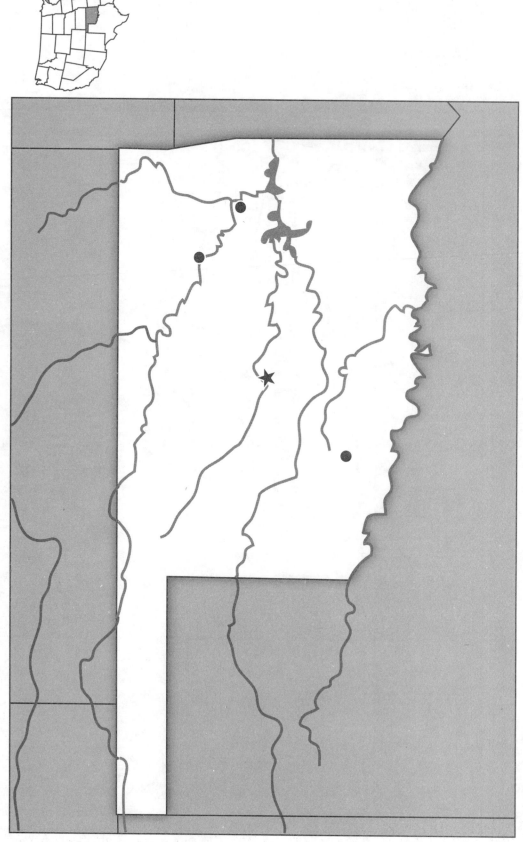

Name: _____

Date: _____

Oregon

WASHINGTON

IDAHO

NEVADA

CALIFORNIA

OREGON

PACIFIC OCEAN

Portland

SALEM

Eugene

Bend

Columbia R.

Deschutes R.

Snake R.

Willamette R.

Umpqua R.

Klamath Lake

Klamath R.

Rogue R.

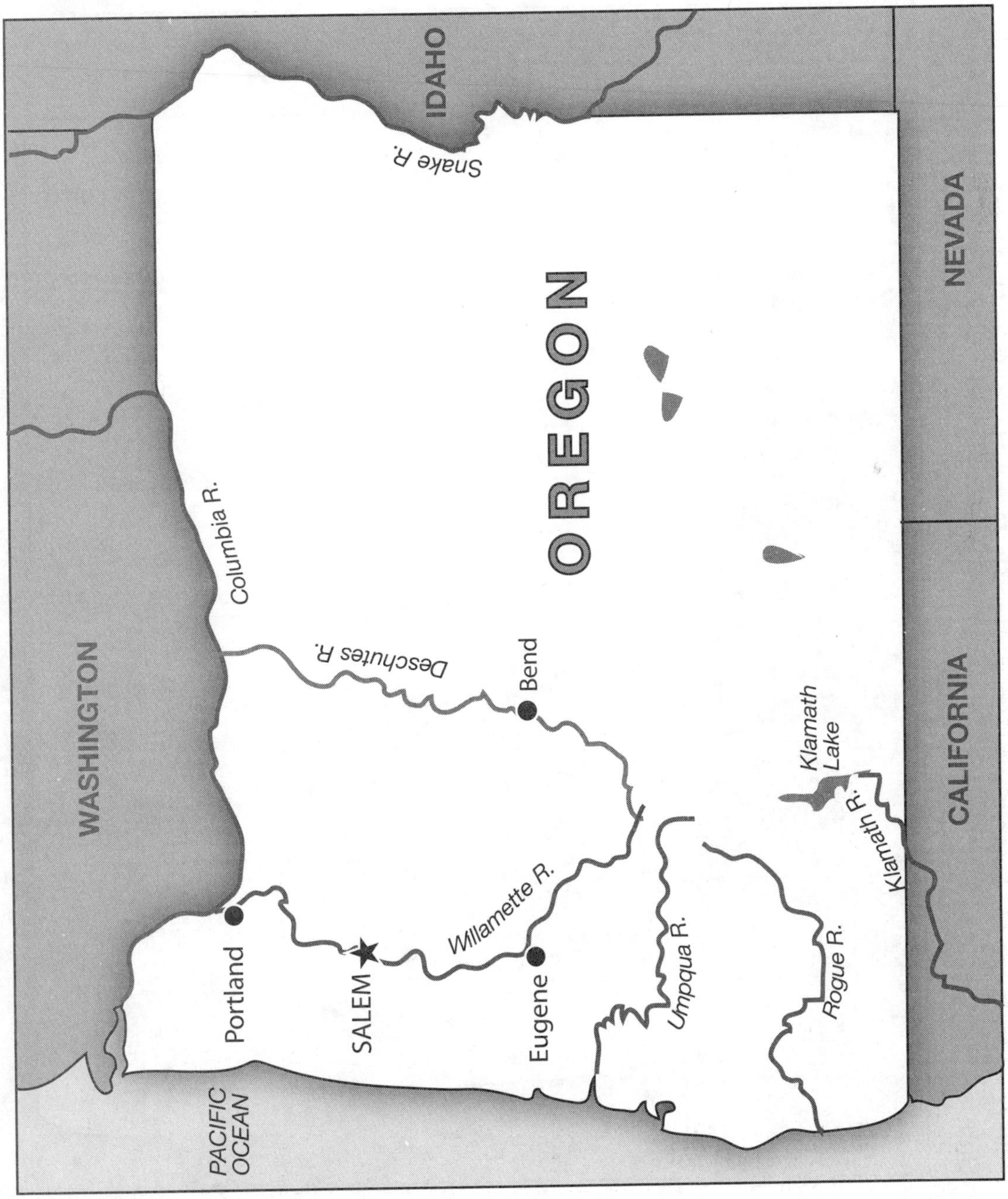

Name: _____

Date: _____

Oregon Map Worksheet

Directions: Label the map with the following:

Cities—Bend, Eugene, Portland, Salem

Rivers—Columbia R., Deschutes R., Klamath R., Rogue R., Snake R., Umpqua R., Willamette R.

States—California, Idaho, Nevada, Oregon, Washington

Bodies of Water—Klamath Lake, Pacific Ocean

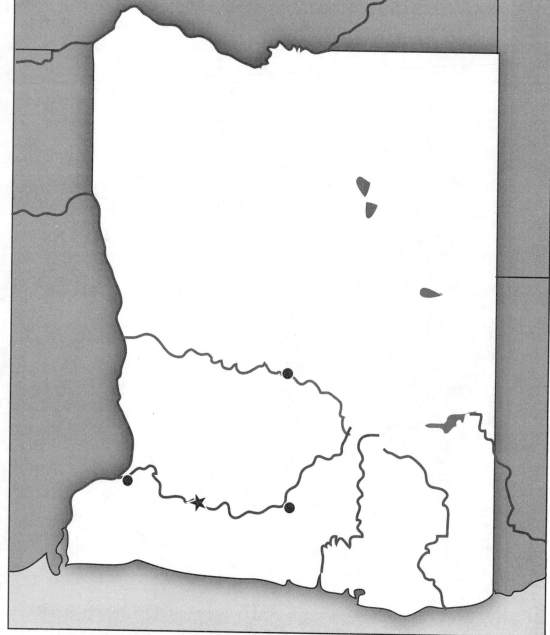

Name: _____

Date: _____

Pennsylvania

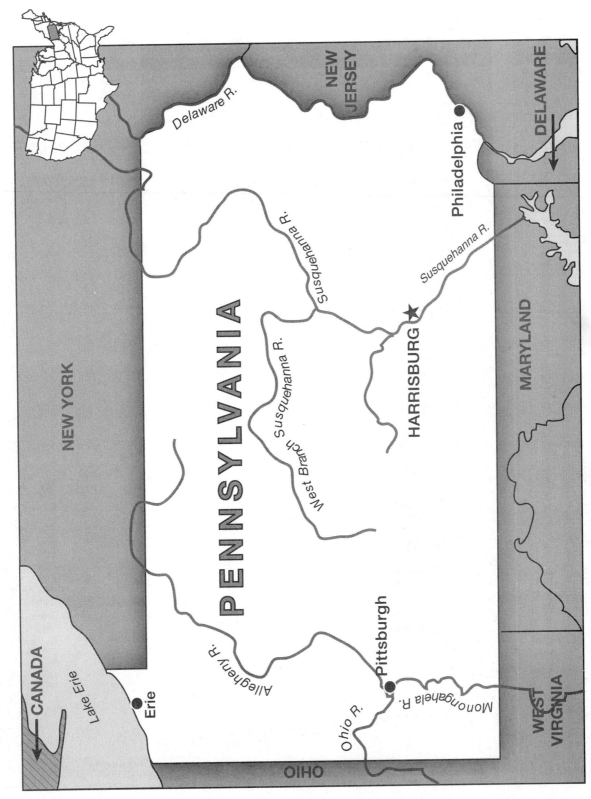

Name: _____ Date: _____

Pennsylvania Map Worksheet

Directions: Label the map with the following:

Cities—Erie, Harrisburg, Philadelphia, Pittsburgh   Body of Water—Lake Erie

Rivers—Allegheny R., Delaware R., Monongahela R., Ohio R., Susquehanna R., West Branch Susquehanna R.

States—Delaware, Maryland, New Jersey, New York, Ohio, Pennyslvania, West Virginia   Country—Canada

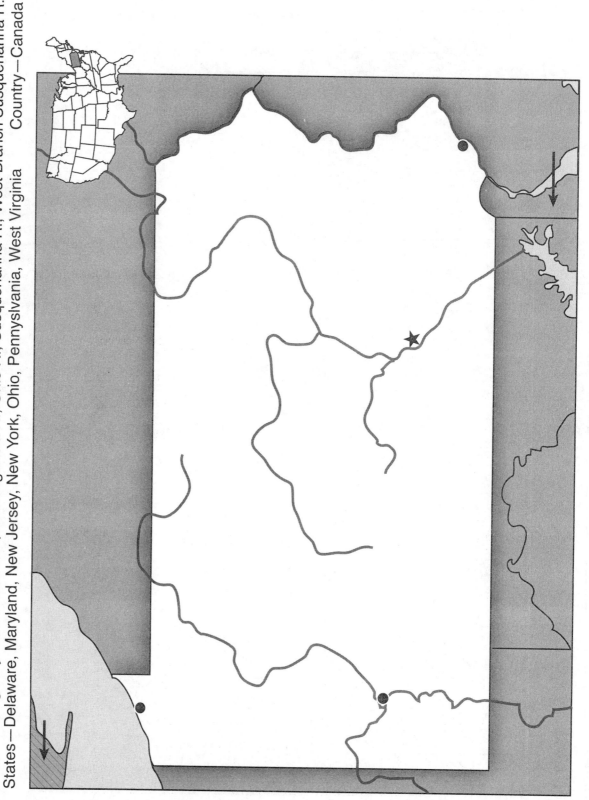

Name: _____

Date: _____

Rhode Island

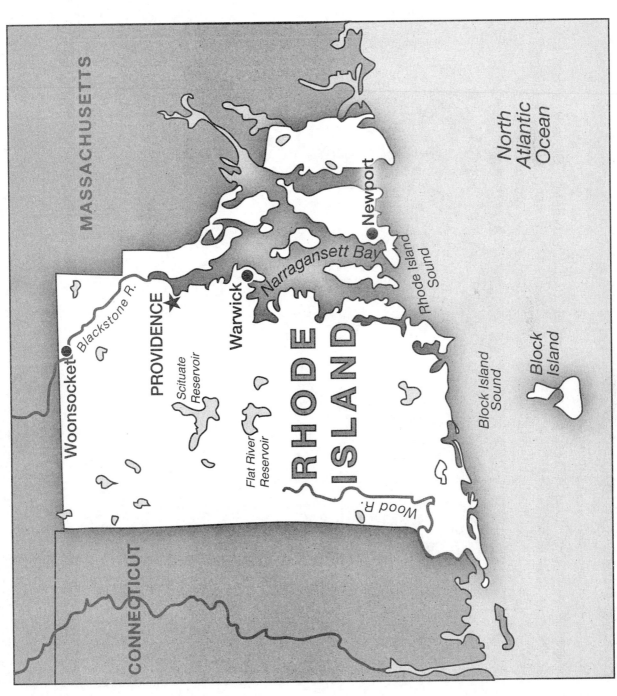

MASSACHUSETTS

CONNECTICUT

North Atlantic Ocean

Woonsocket

Blackstone R.

PROVIDENCE

Scituate Reservoir

Flat River Reservoir

Warwick

Newport

Narragansett Bay

Rhode Island Sound

RHODE ISLAND

Wood R.

Block Island Sound

Block Island

Name: _____

Date: _____

Rhode Island Map Worksheet

Directions: Label the map with the following:

Cities—Newport, Providence, Warwick, Woonsocket　　　Landform—Block Island

Rivers—Blackstone R., Wood R.　　　Bodies of Water—Block Island Sound, Flat River Reservoir, Narragansett Bay,

North Atlantic Ocean, Rhode Island Sound, Scituate Reservoir　　　States—Connecticut, Massachusetts, Rhode Island

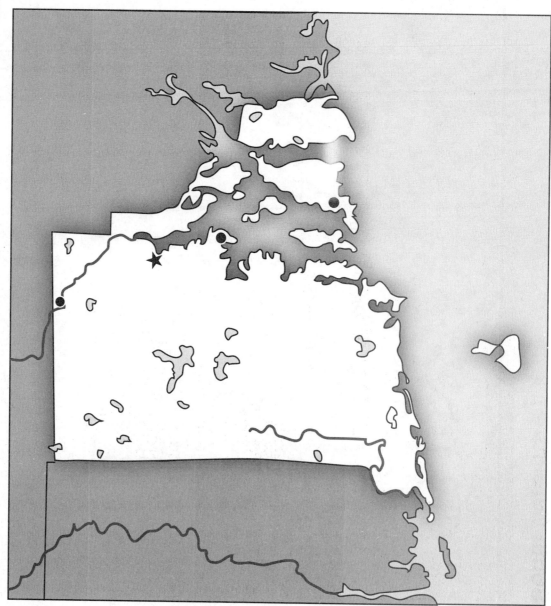

Name: _____

Date: _____

South Carolina

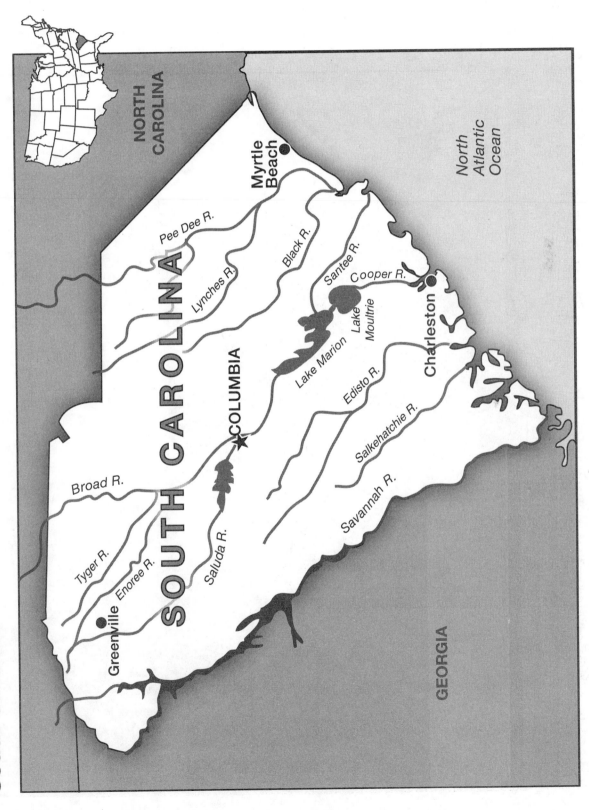

NORTH CAROLINA

North Atlantic Ocean

Myrtle Beach

Pee Dee R.

Black R.

Lynches R.

Santee R.

Cooper R.

SOUTH CAROLINA

Lake Marion

Lake Moultrie

Charleston

Edisto R.

COLUMBIA

Salkehatchie R.

Broad R.

Savannah R.

Tyger R.

Enoree R.

Saluda R.

Greenville

GEORGIA

Name: _____

Date: _____

South Carolina Map Worksheet

Directions: Label the map with the following:

Cities—Charleston, Columbia, Greenville, Myrtle Beach

States—Georgia, North Carolina, South Carolina

Rivers—Black R., Broad R., Cooper R., Edisto R., Enoree R., Lynches R., Pee Dee R., Salkehatchie R., Saluda R., Santee R., Savannah R., Tyger R.

Bodies of Water—Lake Marion, Lake Moultrie, North Atlantic Ocean

Name: _____

Date: _____

South Dakota

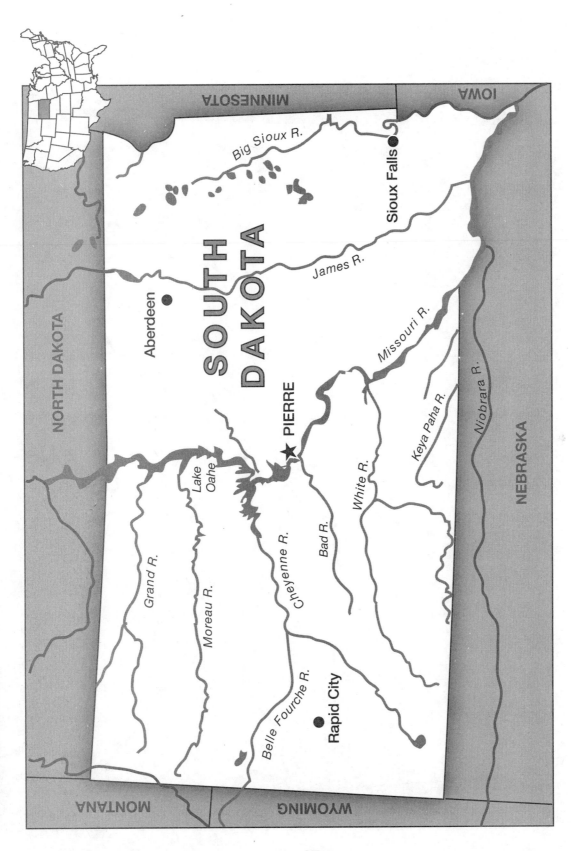

Name: _____

Date: _____

South Dakota Map Worksheet

Directions: Label the map with the following:

Cities—Aberdeen, Pierre, Rapid City, Sioux Falls

Rivers—Bad R., Belle Fourche R., Big Sioux R., Cheyenne R., Grand R., James R., Keya Paha R., Missouri R., Moreau R., Niobrara R., White R.   Body of Water—Lake Oahe

States—Iowa, Minnesota, Montana, Nebraska, North Dakota, South Dakota, Wyoming

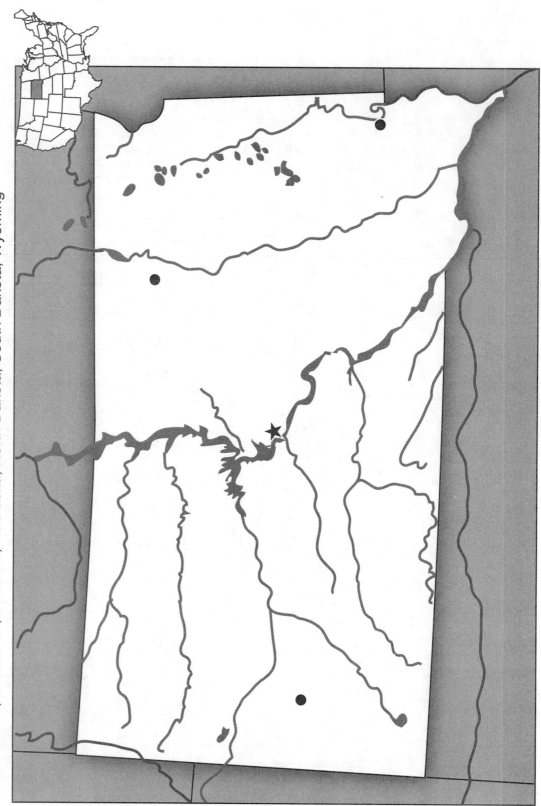

Tennessee

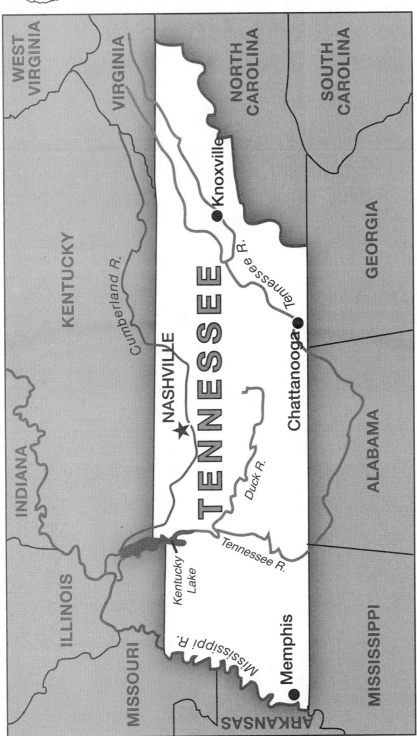

Name: _____

Date: _____

Tennessee Map Worksheet

Directions: Label the map with the following:

Cities—Chattanooga, Knoxville, Memphis, Nashville

Rivers—Cumberland R., Duck R., Mississippi R., Tennessee R.   Body of Water—Kentucky Lake

States—Alabama, Arkansas, Georgia, Illinois, Indiana, Kentucky, Mississippi, Missouri, North Carolina, South Carolina, Tennessee, Virginia, West Virginia

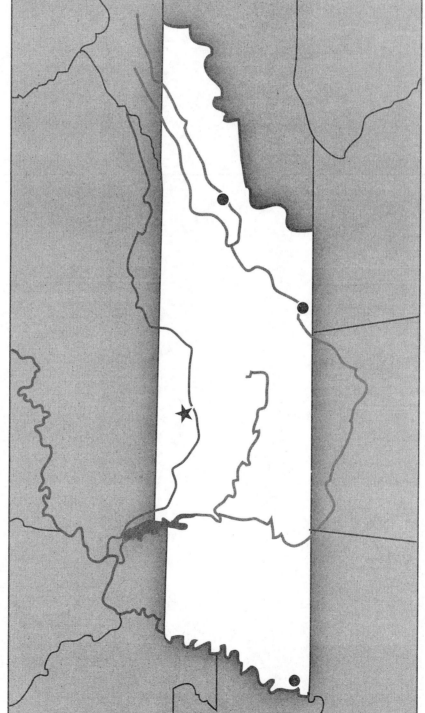

Texas

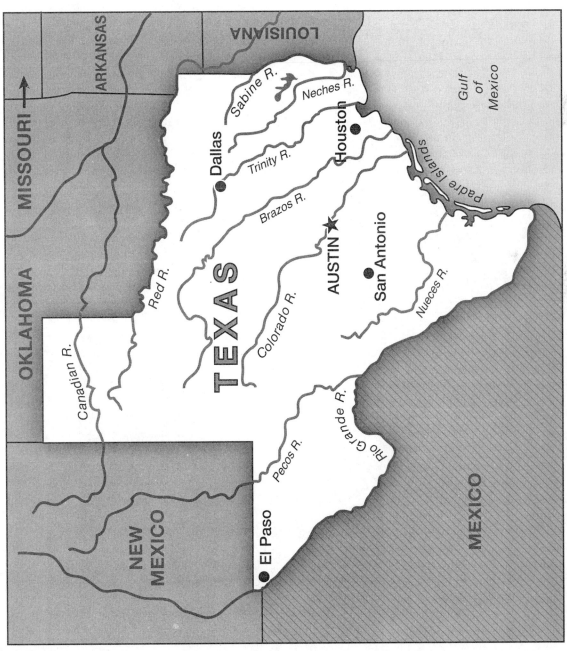

Name: _____

Date: _____

Texas Map Worksheet

Directions: Label the map with the following:

Cities—Austin, Dallas, El Paso, Houston, San Antonio   Landform—Padre Islands   Body of Water—Gulf of Mexico

Rivers—Brazos R., Canadian R., Colorado R., Neches R., Nueces R., Pecos R., Red R., Rio Grande R., Sabine R., Trinity R.

States—Arkansas, Louisiana, Missouri, New Mexico, Oklahoma, Texas   Country—Mexico

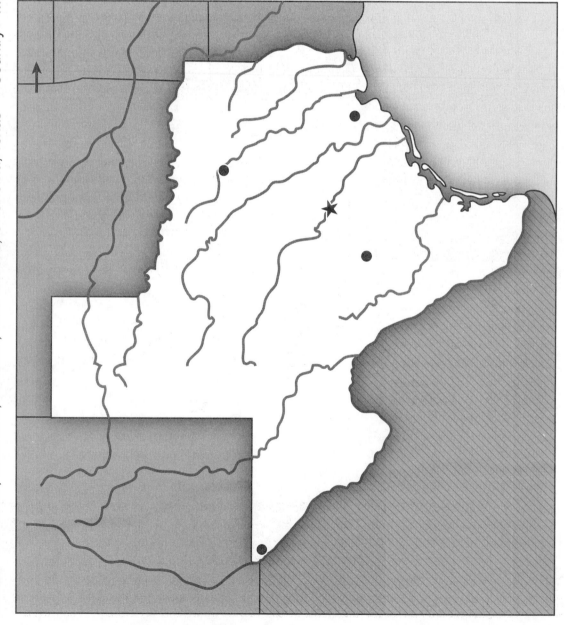

Utah

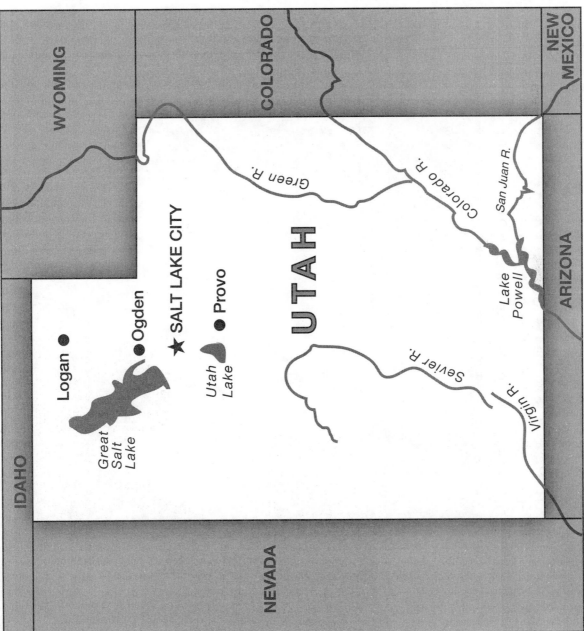

Name: _____

Date: _____

Utah Map Worksheet

Directions: Label the map with the following:

Cities—Logan, Ogden, Provo, Salt Lake City

Rivers—Colorado R., Green R., San Juan R., Sevier R., Virgin R.

Bodies of Water—Great Salt Lake, Lake Powell, Utah Lake

States—Arizona, Colorado, Idaho, Nevada, New Mexico, Utah, Wyoming

Name: _____

Date: _____

Vermont

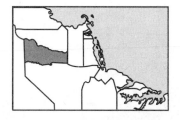

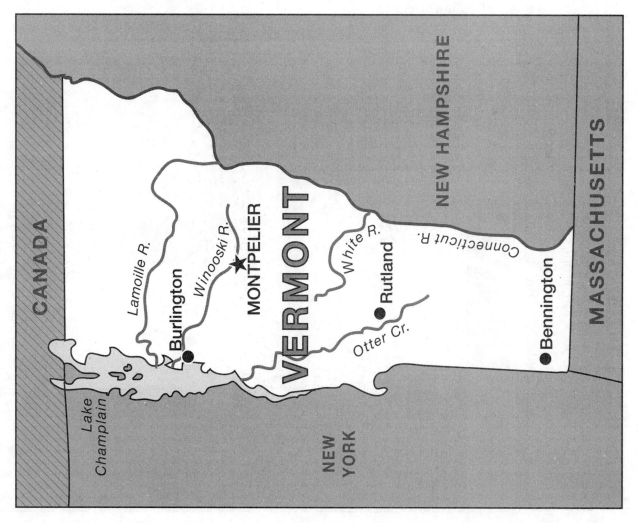

CANADA

Lake Champlain

Lamoille R.

Burlington

Winooski R.

MONTPELIER

VERMONT

White R.

Rutland

Otter Cr.

Connecticut R.

NEW HAMPSHIRE

MASSACHUSETTS

Bennington

NEW YORK

Name: _____   Date: _____

Vermont Map Worksheet

Directions: Label the map with the following:

Cities—Bennington, Burlington, Montpelier, Rutland

Rivers—Connecticut R., Lamoille R., Otter Cr., White R., Winooski R.

States—Massachusetts, New Hampshire, New York, Vermont

Body of Water—Lake Champlain

Country—Canada

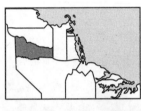

Name: _____

Date: _____

Virginia

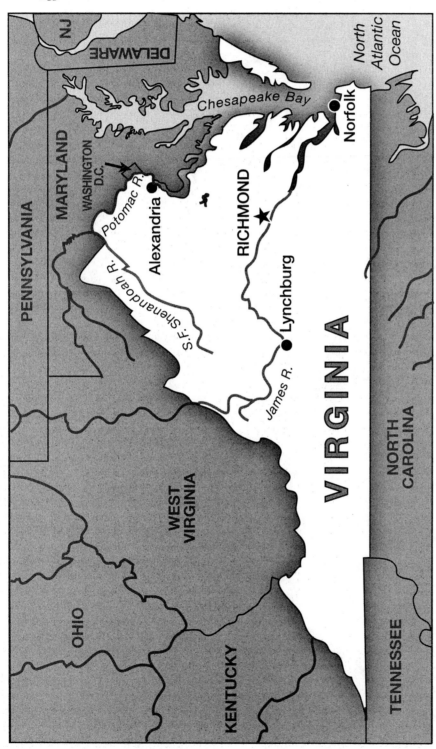

Name: _____

Date: _____

Virginia Map Worksheet

Directions: Label the map with the following:

Cities—Alexandria, Lynchburg, Norfolk, Richmond, Washington, D.C.

Rivers—James R., Potomac R., South Fork Shenandoah R.

Bodies of Water—Chesapeake Bay, North Atlantic Ocean

States—Delaware, Kentucky, Maryland, New Jersey, North Carolina, Ohio, Pennsylvania, Tennessee, Virginia, West Virginia

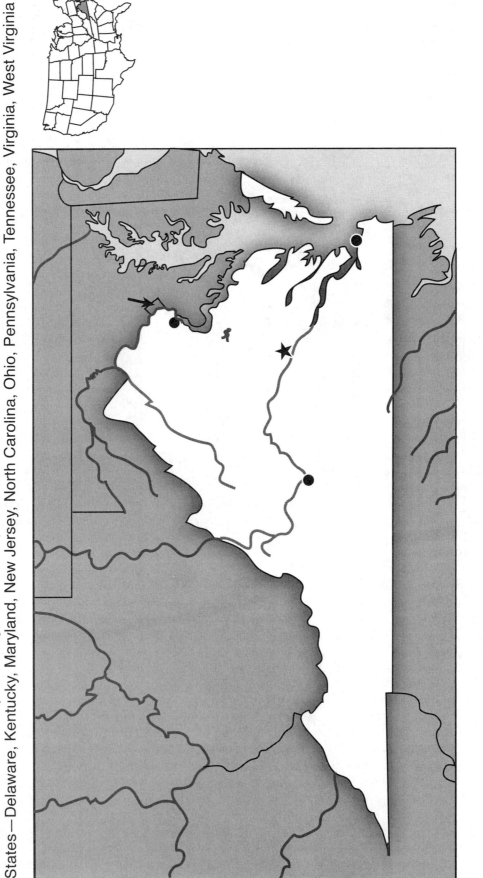

Name: _____

Date: _____

Washington

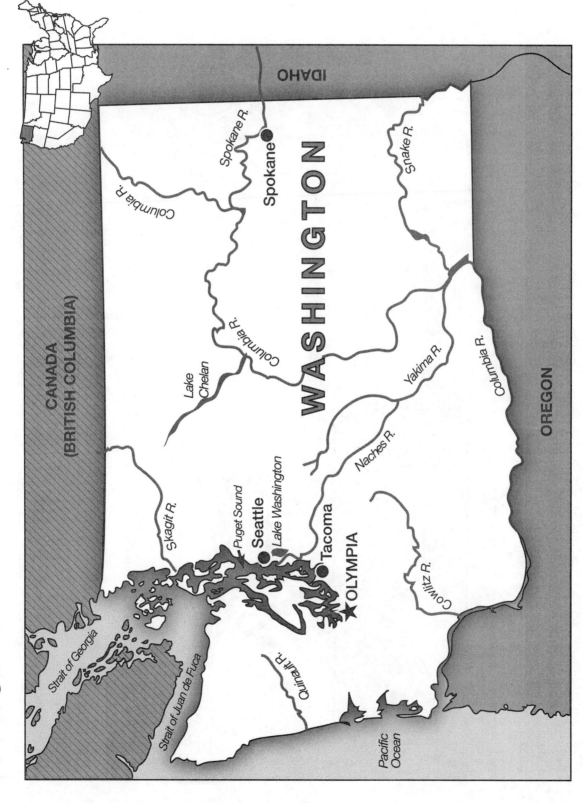

Name: _____

Date: _____

Washington Map Worksheet

Directions: Label the map with the following:

Cities—Olympia, Seattle, Spokane, Tacoma

Rivers—Columbia R., Cowlitz R., Naches R., Quinault R., Skagit R., Snake R., Spokane R., Yakima R.

Bodies of Water—Lake Chelan, Lake Washington, Pacific Ocean, Puget Sound, Strait of Georgia, Strait of Juan de Fuca

States—Idaho, Oregon, Washington   Country—Canada

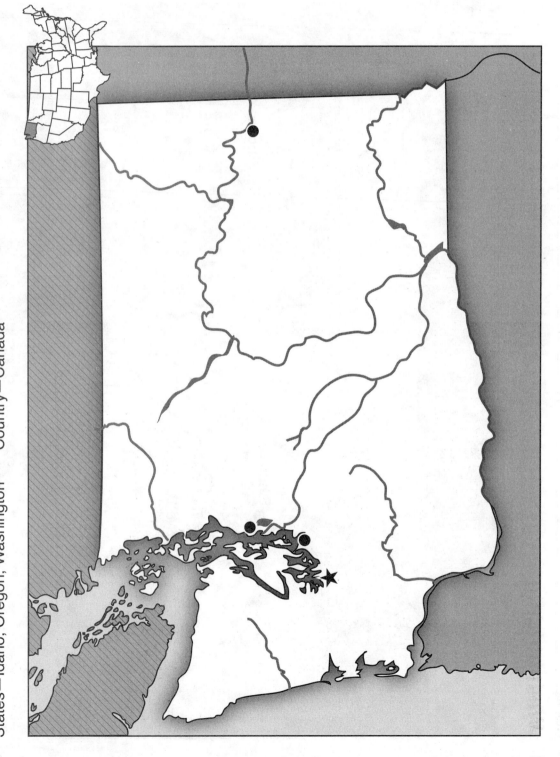

Name: _____

Date: _____

West Virginia

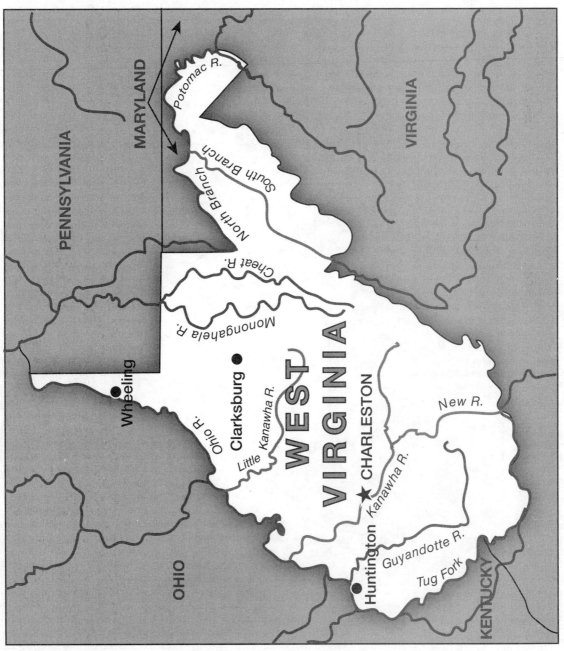

Name: _____

Date: _____

West Virginia Map Worksheet

Directions: Label the map with the following:

Cities—Charleston, Clarksburg, Huntington, Wheeling

Rivers—Guyandotte R., Kanawha R., Little Kanawha R., New R., Ohio R., Potomac R. (North Branch and South Branch)

States—Kentucky, Maryland, Ohio, Pennsylvania, Virginia, West Virginia

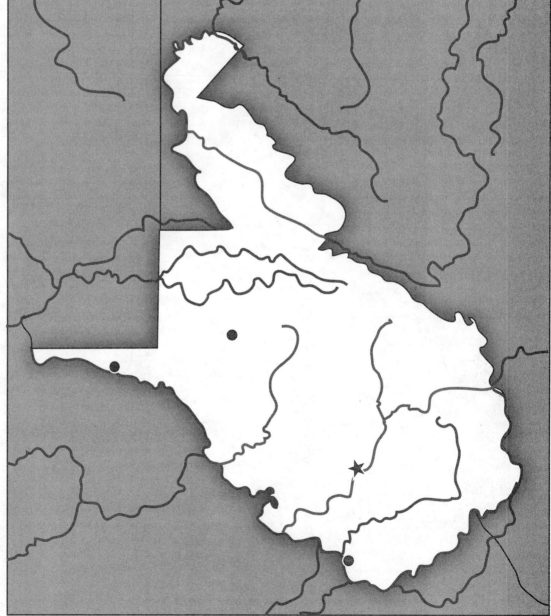

Name:

Date:

Wisconsin

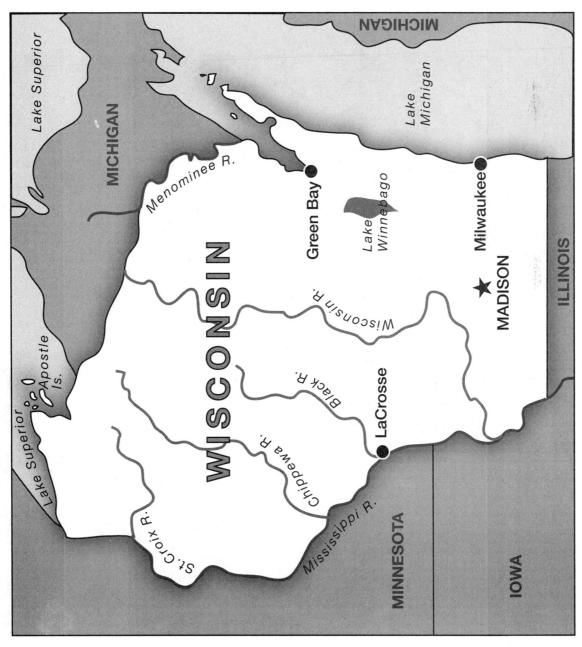

Name: _____

Date: _____

Wisconsin Map Worksheet

Directions: Label the map with the following:

Cities—Green Bay, LaCrosse, Madison, Milwaukee   Landform—Apostle Island

Rivers—Black R., Chippewa R., Menominee R., Mississippi R., St. Croix R., Wisconsin R.

Bodies of Water—Lake Michigan, Lake Superior, Lake Winnebago

States—Illinois, Iowa, Michigan, Minnesota, Wisconsin

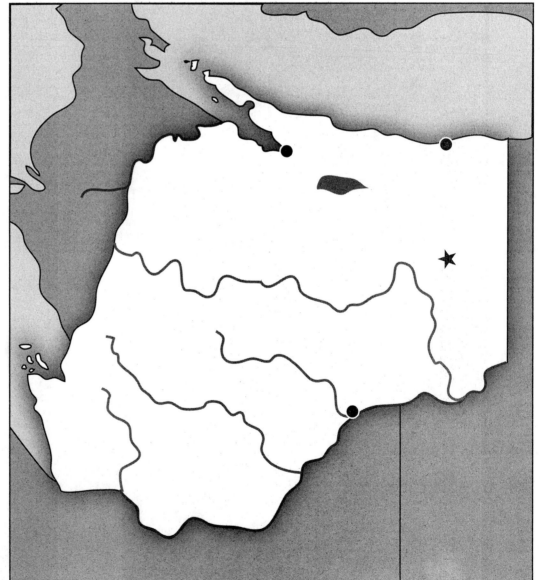

Name: _____

Date: _____

Wyoming

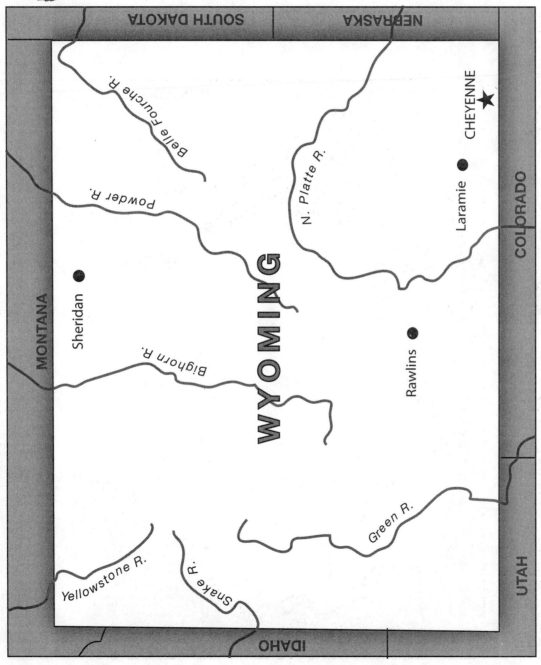

Name: _____

Date: _____

Wyoming Map Worksheet

Directions: Label the map with the following:

Cities—Cheyenne, Laramie, Rawlins, Sheridan

Rivers—Belle Fourche R., Bighorn R., Green R., North Platte R., Powder R., Snake R., Yellowstone R.

States—Colorado, Idaho, Montana, Nebraska, South Dakota, Utah, Wyoming

Name: _____

Date: _____

District of Columbia (Washington, D.C.)

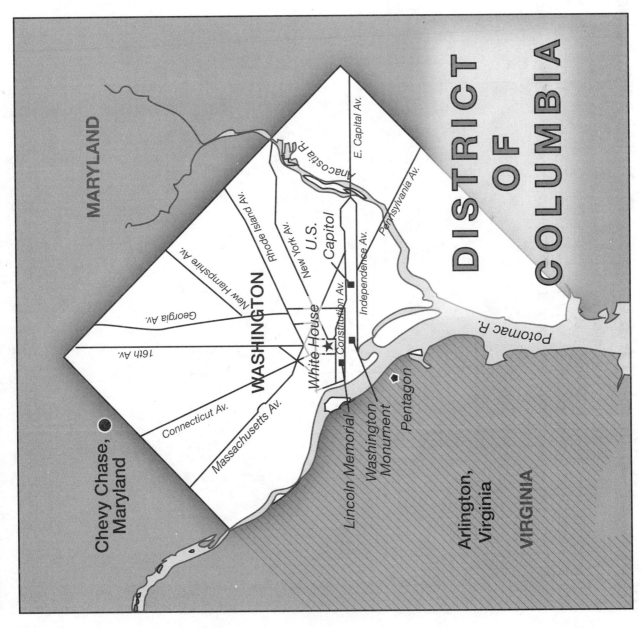

MARYLAND

Chevy Chase,
Maryland

WASHINGTON

New Hampshire Av.

Georgia Av.

16th Av.

Connecticut Av.

Massachusetts Av.

Rhode Island Av.

New York Av.

U.S.
Capitol

White House

Constitution Av.

Independence Av.

Anacostia R.

E. Capital Av.

Pennsylvania Av.

Lincoln Memorial

Washington
Monument

Pentagon

Potomac R.

DISTRICT
OF
COLUMBIA

Arlington, Virginia

VIRGINIA

Name: _____

Date: _____

District of Columbia (Washington, D.C.) Map Worksheet

Directions: Label the map with the following:

Cities—Arlington, VA; Chevy Chase, MD; Washington, D.C.

Rivers—Anacostia R., Potomac R.   States—Maryland, Virginia

Landmarks—Lincoln Memorial, Pentagon, U.S. Capitol, Washington Monument, White House

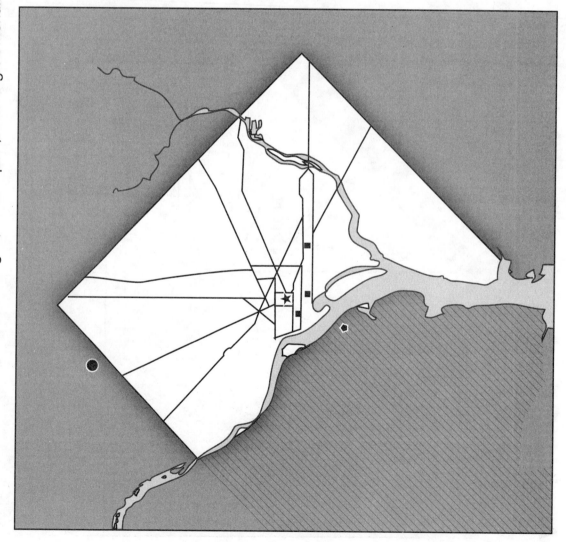

Name: _____

Date: _____

American Samoa

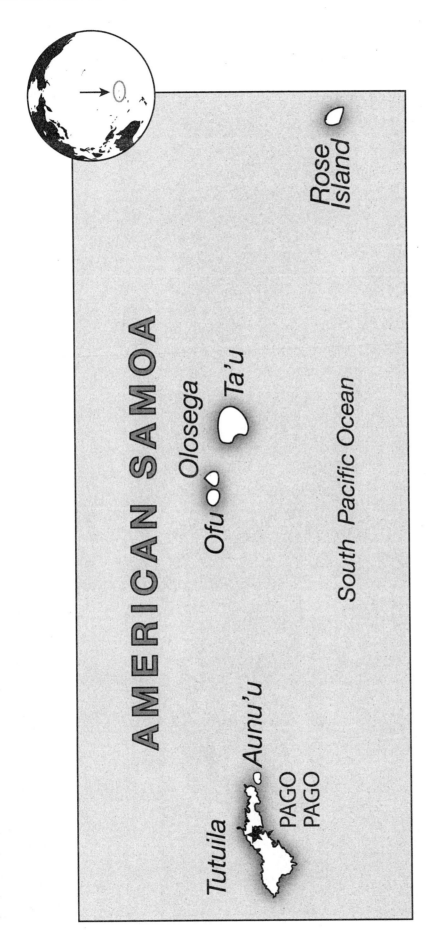

AMERICAN SAMOA

Olosega

Ta'u

Ofu

Rose Island

Tutuila

Aunu'u

PAGO PAGO

South Pacific Ocean

Name: _____

Date: _____

American Samoa Map Worksheet

Directions: Label the map with the following:

Cities—Pago Pago

Islands—Aunu'u, Ofu, Olosega, Rose Island, Ta'u, Tutuila

Body of Water—South Pacific Ocean

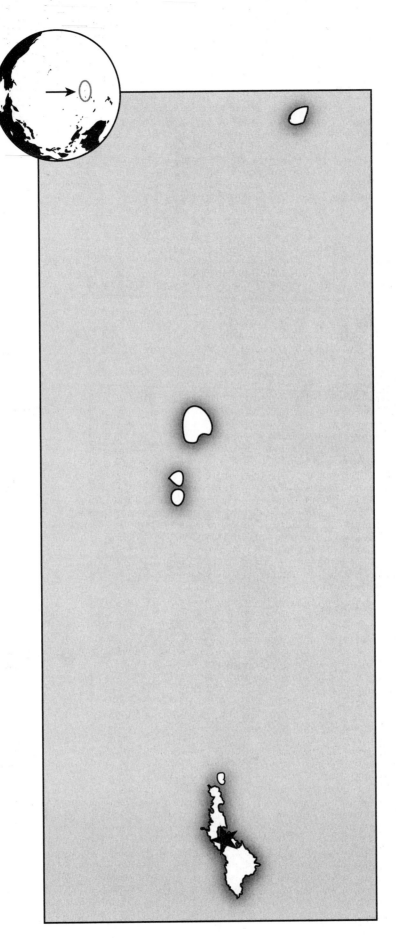

Name:

Date:

Guam

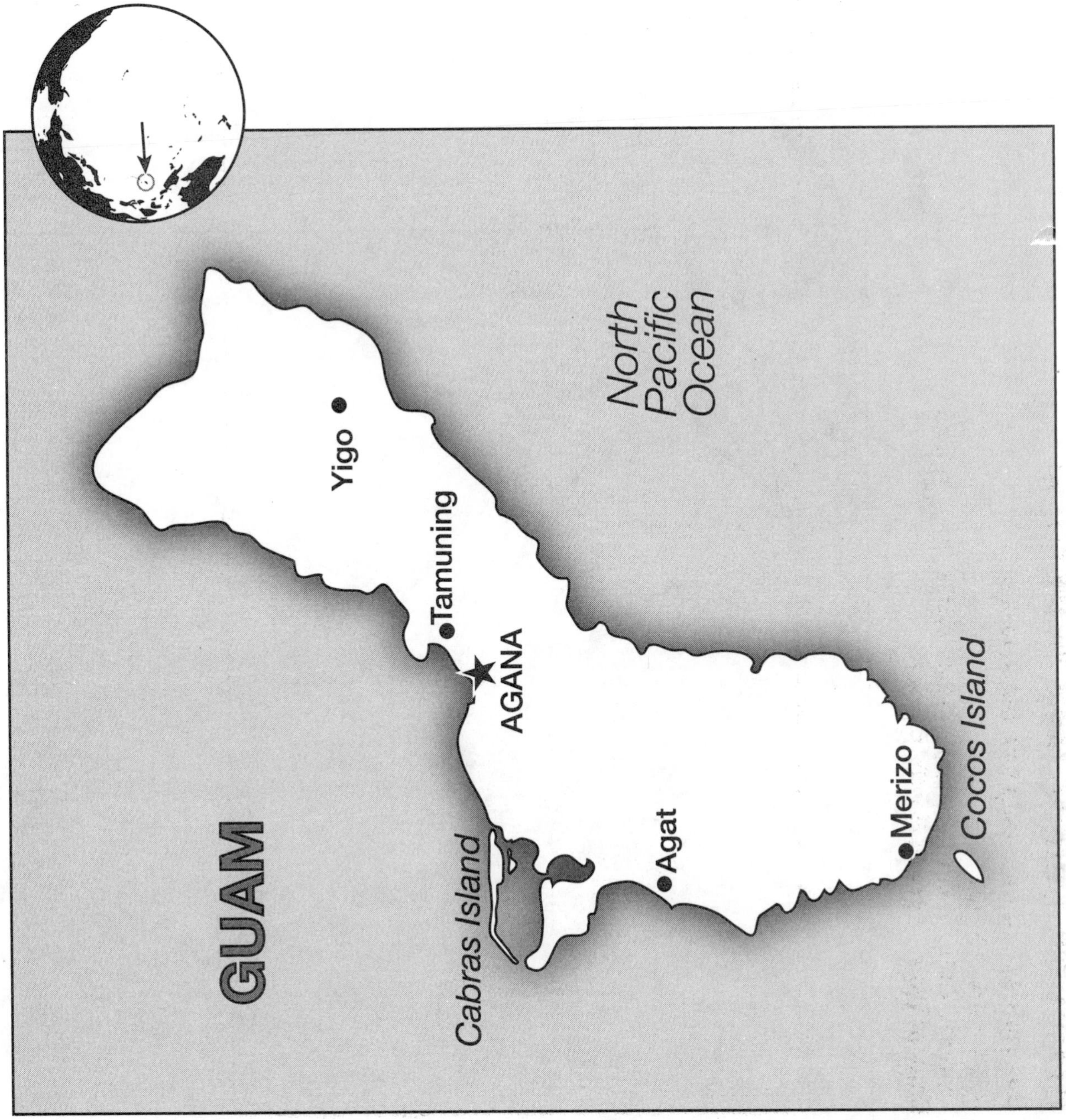

GUAM

Yigo

Tamuning

AGANA

Cabras Island

Agat

Merizo

Cocos Island

North Pacific Ocean

Name: _____

Date: _____

Guam Map Worksheet

Directions: Label the map with the following:
Cities—Agana, Agat, Merizo, Tamuning, Yigo
Islands—Cabras Island, Cocos Island, Guam
Body of Water—North Pacific Ocean

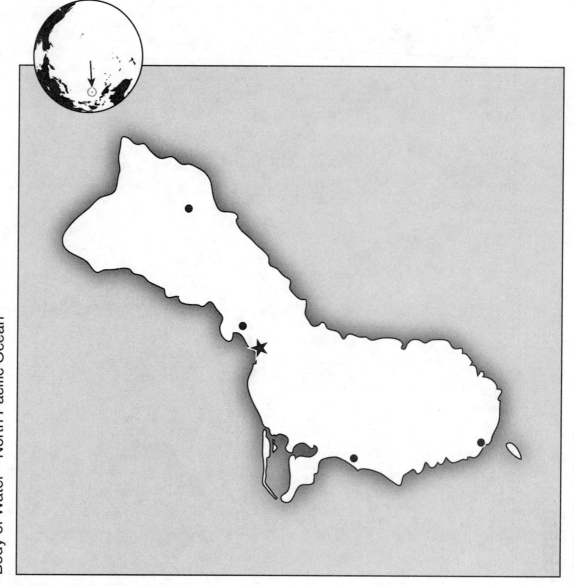

Northern Marianas Islands

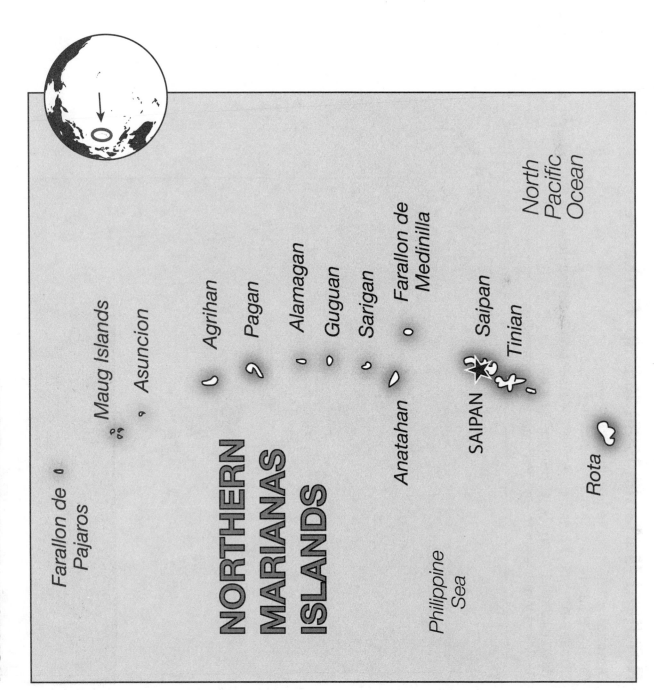

NORTHERN MARIANAS ISLANDS

Farallon de Pajaros

Maug Islands

Asuncion

Agrihan

Pagan

Alamagan

Guguan

Sarigan

Farallon de Medinilla

Anatahan

Saipan

SAIPAN

Tinian

Rota

North Pacific Ocean

Philippine Sea

Name: _____

Date: _____

Northern Marianas Islands Map Worksheet

Directions: Label the map with the following:

Cities—Saipan

Islands—Agrihan, Alamagan, Anatahan, Asuncion, Farallon de Medinilla, Farallon de Pajaros, Guguan, Maug Islands, Pagan, Rota, Saipan, Sarigan, Tinian

Bodies of Water—North Pacific Ocean, Philippine Sea

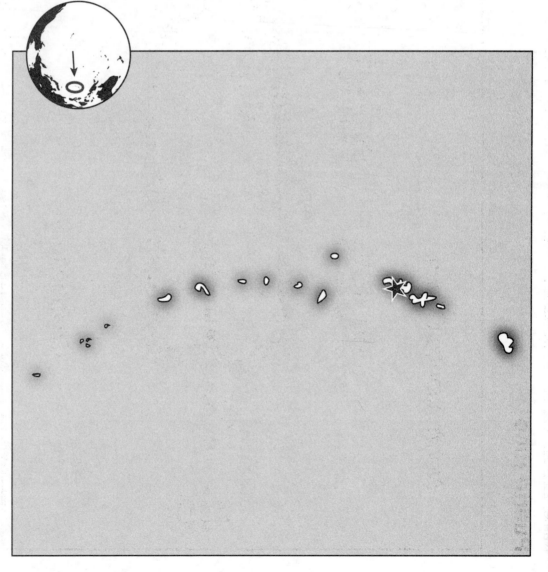

Name: _____

Date: _____

Puerto Rico

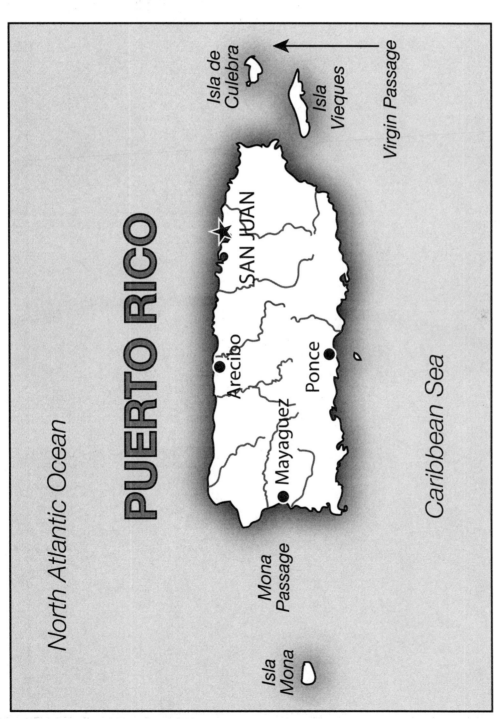

North Atlantic Ocean

PUERTO RICO

Isla de Culebra

Isla Vieques

Virgin Passage

SAN JUAN

Arecibo

Ponce

Mayaguez

Caribbean Sea

Mona Passage

Isla Mona

Name: _____

Date: _____

Puerto Rico Map Worksheet

Directions: Label the map with the following:

Cities—Arecibo, Mayaguez, Ponce, San Juan

Islands—Isla de Culebra, Isla Mona, Isla Vieques, Puerto Rico

Bodies of Water—Caribbean Sea, Mona Passage, North Atlantic Ocean, Virgin Passage

U.S. Virgin Islands

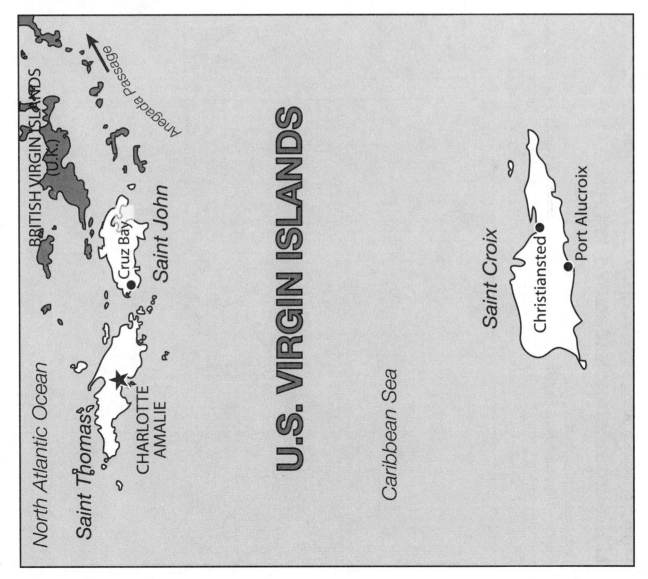

North Atlantic Ocean

BRITISH VIRGIN ISLANDS (U.K.)

Anegada Passage

Saint Thomas

CHARLOTTE AMALIE

Cruz Bay

Saint John

U.S. VIRGIN ISLANDS

Caribbean Sea

Saint Croix

Christiansted

Port Alucroix

Name: _____ Date: _____

U.S. Virgin Islands Map Worksheet

Directions: Label the map with the following:

Cities—Charlotte Amalie, Christiansted, Cruz Bay, Port Alucroix

Islands—Saint Croix, Saint John, Saint Thomas, British Virgin Islands (U.K.)

Bodies of Water—Anegada Passage, Caribbean Sea, North Atlantic Ocean

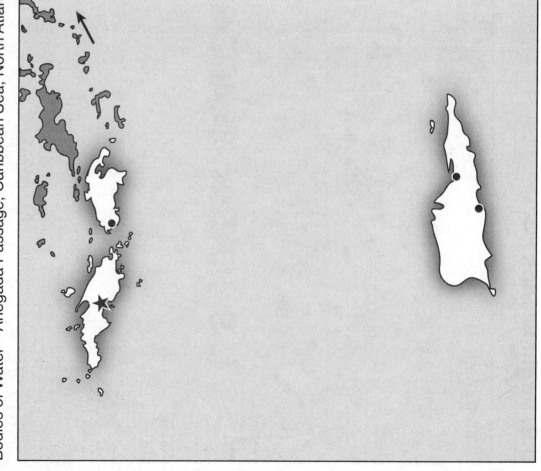

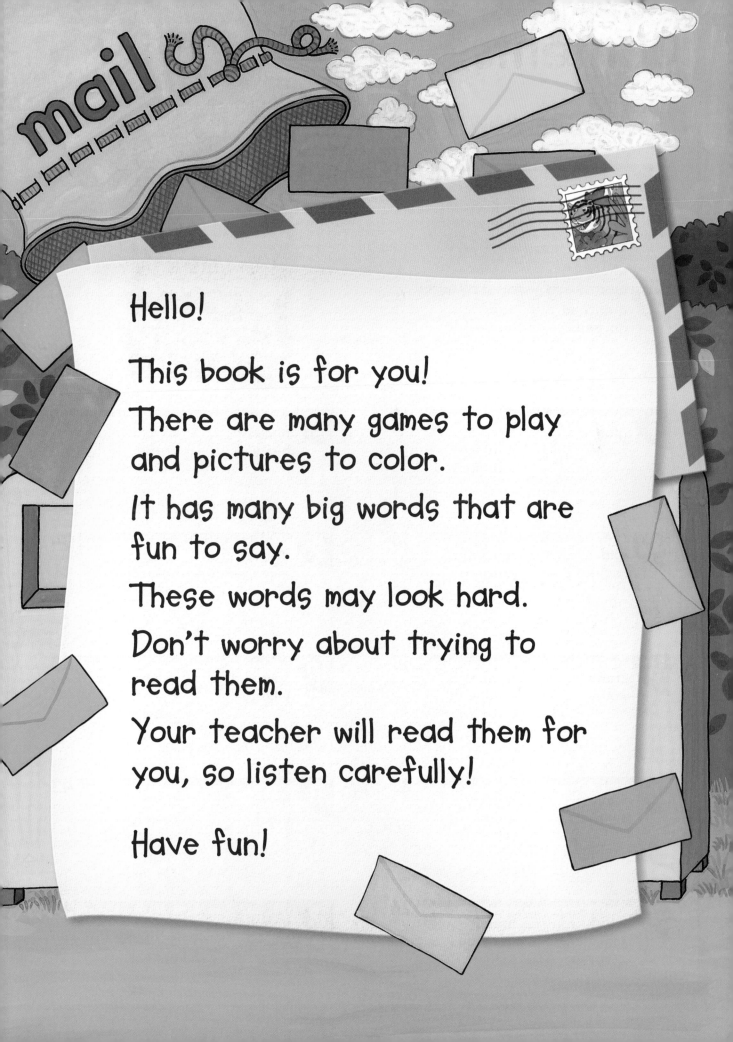

Hello!

This book is for you!

There are many games to play and pictures to color.

It has many big words that are fun to say.

These words may look hard.

Don't worry about trying to read them.

Your teacher will read them for you, so listen carefully!

Have fun!

Contents

1 glimmer

2 fleet

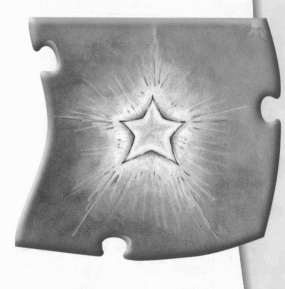

3 comforting

Teacher: For each numbered item, read the vocabulary word aloud. Ask children to draw a line to connect pictures that show the same word. Then ask children to explain why they connected the pictures they did.

Listen. Color.

1

lively

2

expression

Teacher: For each numbered item, read the vocabulary word aloud. Ask children to color the picture or pictures that match the word. Then ask children to tell which pictures they colored and why.

3

1 Which picture shows something **lively**?

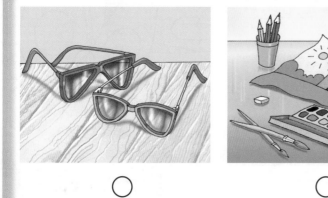

○　　　　　　　○　　　　　　　○

2 Which picture shows a parent **comforting** someone?

○　　　　　　　○　　　　　　　○

Teacher: Read aloud each numbered item and have children fill in the bubble under the best picture.

3 Which picture shows something that **glimmers**?

◯ ◯ ◯

4 Which child's **expression** can you see?

◯ ◯ ◯

5 Which picture shows a **fleet** goose?

◯ ◯ ◯

5

Listen. Color.

1

drenched

2

gorgeous

Teacher: For each numbered item, read the vocabulary word aloud. Ask children to color the picture or pictures that match the word. Then ask children to tell which pictures they colored and why.

Listen. Draw.

vain
linger
peculiar

Teacher: Ask children to look at the zoo pictures and tell what they see. Have them draw a box around the animal or person who is **vain**. Have them draw a line under the child who wants to **linger**. Then ask children to draw a circle around the most **peculiar** animal. Ask children to tell which pictures they marked and why.

7

1 Which picture shows someone who **lingers**?

○   ○   ○

2 Which picture shows something **gorgeous**?

○   ○   ○

Teacher: Read aloud each numbered item and have children fill in the bubble under the best picture.

3 Which picture shows something **peculiar**?

○ ○ ○

4 Which picture shows boys who are **drenched**?

○ ○ ○

5 Which picture shows someone who is **vain**?

○ ○ ○

Listen. Draw.

1 timid

2 frantic

3 glance

Teacher: For each numbered item, read the vocabulary word aloud. Ask children to draw a line to connect pictures that show the same word. Then ask children to explain why they connected the pictures they did.

Listen. Color.

1

intimidated

2

reluctant

Teacher: For each numbered item, read the vocabulary word aloud. Ask children to color the picture or pictures that match the word. Then ask children to tell which pictures they colored and why.

11

1 Which picture shows something that might **intimidate** you?

○   ○   ○

2 Which picture shows a time when you might **glance** at something?

○   ○   ○

Teacher: Read aloud each numbered item and have children fill in the bubble under the best picture.

3 Which picture shows someone who is **timid**?

○   ○   ○

4 Which picture shows something you might be **reluctant** to touch?

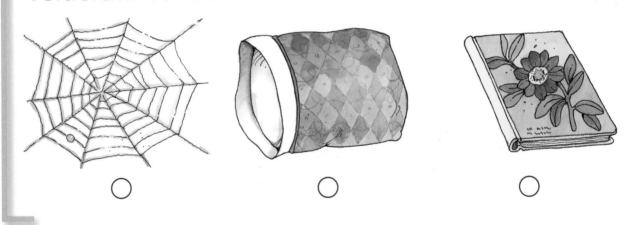

○   ○   ○

5 Which picture shows someone who is **frantic**?

○   ○   ○

13

Listen. Draw.

1 glide

2 soar

Teacher: For each numbered item, read the vocabulary word aloud. Ask children to draw a line through the pictures that show the word in some way. Then ask children to tell why they connected the pictures they did.

Listen. Draw.

1 journey

2 roam

3 adventure

Teacher: For each numbered item, read the vocabulary word aloud. Ask children to draw a line to connect pictures that show the same word. Then ask children to explain why they connected the pictures they did.

1 Which picture shows an **adventure**?

○   ○   ○

2 Which bird is **soaring**?

○   ○   ○

Teacher: Read aloud each numbered item and have children fill in the bubble under the best picture.

3 Which might someone use to **roam**?

○   ○   ○

4 Which would you ride to take a **journey**?

○   ○   ○

5 Which picture shows a person **gliding**?

○   ○   ○

Listen. Draw.

1 lounge

2 stumble

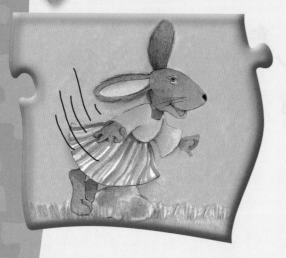

3 pursue

Teacher: For each numbered item, read the vocabulary word aloud. Then ask children to draw a line to connect pictures that show the same word. Then ask children to explain why they connected the pictures they did.

Listen. Color.

1 collide

2 absurd

3 lounge

Teacher: For each numbered item, read the vocabulary word aloud. Ask children to color the picture or pictures that match the word. Then ask children to tell which pictures they colored and why.

19

1 Which picture shows a boy **stumbling**?

◯   ◯   ◯

2 Which picture shows a woman **pursuing** something?

◯   ◯   ◯

Teacher: Read aloud each numbered item and have children fill in the bubble under the best picture.

3 Which picture shows children **colliding**?

○ ○ ○

4 Which picture shows an **absurd** rabbit?

○ ○ ○

5 Which picture shows a girl **lounging**?

○ ○ ○

Listen. Draw.

1 swirl

2 wavy

Teacher: For each numbered item, read the vocabulary word aloud. Ask children to draw a line through the pictures that show the word in some way. Then ask children to tell why they connected the pictures they did.

Listen. Draw.

relief

alert

narrow

23

1 Which picture shows a hiker on a **narrow** path?

○   ○   ○

2 Which picture shows a child **swirling**?

○   ○   ○

Teacher: Read aloud each numbered item and have children fill in the bubble under the best picture.

3 Which picture shows a worker who feels **relief**?

◯   ◯   ◯

4 Which picture shows an **alert** cat?

◯   ◯   ◯

5 Which box is wrapped in a **wavy** pattern?

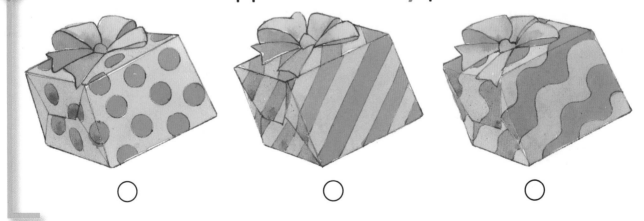

◯   ◯   ◯

1 whisk

2 scamper

3 describe

Teacher: For each numbered item, read the vocabulary word aloud. Ask children to color the picture or pictures that match the word. Then ask children to tell which pictures they colored and why.

Listen. Color.

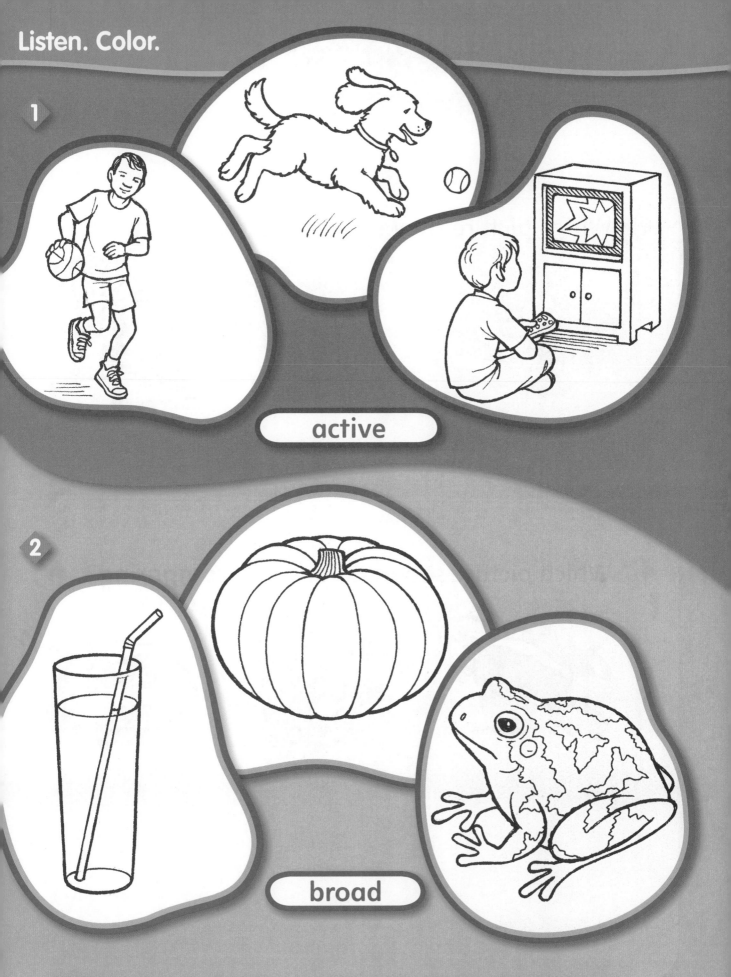

1

active

2

broad

1 Which picture shows someone being **active**?

◯   ◯   ◯

2 Which picture shows an animal **scampering**?

◯   ◯   ◯

Teacher: Read aloud each numbered item and have children fill in the bubble under the best picture.

3 Which could you use to **whisk** something?

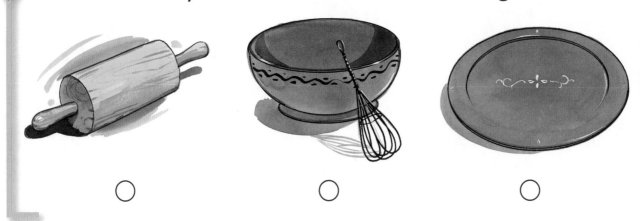

○   ○   ○

4 Which picture shows something that is **broad**?

○   ○   ○

5 Which person is **describing** something?

○   ○   ○

Listen. Draw.

observe

mischievous

Teacher: Ask children to look at the picture and tell what they see. Have them draw a circle around the child who is **observing**. Then ask children to draw a box around the person who is being **mischievous**. Ask children to tell which pictures they marked and why.

Listen. Draw.

1 hefty

2 ancient

Teacher: For each numbered item, read the vocabulary word aloud. Ask children to draw a line through the pictures that show the word in some way. Then ask children to tell why they connected the pictures they did.

31

1 Which animal is **ancient**?

◯ ◯ ◯

2 Which picture shows someone **observing** a lion?

◯ ◯ ◯

3 Which picture shows a **mischievous** bear?

○ ○ ○

4 Which picture shows something **hefty**?

○ ○ ○

5 In which picture is the girl **tracking** a frog?

○ ○ ○

Listen. Color. Draw.

discouraged
extraordinary
desire

Teacher: Ask children to color red the T-shirt of the child who is **discouraged**. Ask them to color blue the T-shirt of the child who is wearing an **extraordinary** hat. Then have children draw in the thought bubble what the kitten **desires**. Ask children to tell which pictures they colored, what they drew, and why.

34

Listen. Draw.

1 hesitate

2 respect

3 extraordinary

Teacher: For each numbered item, read the vocabulary word aloud. Ask children to draw a line to connect pictures that show the same word. Then ask children to explain why they connected the pictures they did.

35

1 Which picture shows a **discouraged** boy?

○   ○   ○

2 Which picture shows a dog getting something it **desires**?

○   ○   ○

Teacher: Read aloud each numbered item and have children fill in the bubble under the best picture.

3 Which picture shows someone **hesitating**?

○   ○   ○

4 Which picture shows a boy showing **respect**?

○   ○   ○

5 Which picture shows an **extraordinary** apple?

○   ○   ○

Listen. Draw.

village

Teacher: Direct children to the hiker at the top of the path and the cabin near the bottom. Ask children to help the hiker find his cabin by drawing a line through the **villages**. Then ask children to tell which path they chose and why.

Listen. Draw.

splendid
celebrate
option

Teacher: Ask children to look at the picnic scene and tell what they see. Then ask children to draw a circle around the dog that is having a **splendid** time. Have them draw a line under the children who are **celebrating**. Ask them to draw a box around the child who has food **options**. Then ask children to tell which pictures they marked and why.

1 In which picture is a little rabbit showing that she **appreciates** her grandmother?

○   ○   ○

2 Which picture shows something **splendid**?

○   ○   ○

Teacher: Read aloud each numbered item and have children fill in the bubble under the best picture.

3 Which picture shows a **village**?

○   ○   ○

4 Which picture shows an **option**?

○   ○   ○

5 Where would people most likely **celebrate**?

○   ○   ○

Listen. Draw.

displeased

Teacher: Direct children to the cat at the bottom of the path and the grocery store at the top. Ask children to help the cat get to the store by drawing a line through the animals that are **displeased**. Then ask children to tell which pictures they drew a line through and why.

Listen. Color.

1 amble

2 bare

3 fetch

Teacher: For each numbered item, read the vocabulary word aloud. Ask children to color the picture or pictures that match the word. Then ask children to tell which pictures they colored and why.

43

1 Which picture shows a **bare** desk?

○ ○ ○

2 Which picture shows a young elephant making a **request**?

○ ○ ○

Teacher: Read aloud each numbered item and have children fill in the bubble under the best picture.

3 Which picture shows a frog **fetching** a ball?

○   ○   ○

4 Which picture shows a cat **ambling**?

○   ○   ○

5 Which picture shows a **displeased** clown?

○   ○   ○

unlikely

perilous

Teacher: Ask children to color blue the shoes of the person who is **unlikely** to be in a circus parade. Ask them to color brown the dog that is in a **perilous** place. Then ask children to tell which pictures they colored and why.

Listen. Draw.

pounce

nestle

snare

Teacher: Ask children to look at the zoo scene and tell what they see. Then ask children to draw a circle around the animal that is **pouncing**. Have them draw a line under the animals that are **nestling**. Ask them to draw a box around the adult who is trying to **snare** an animal. Ask children to tell which pictures they marked and why.

1 Which picture shows a lizard in a **perilous** situation?

  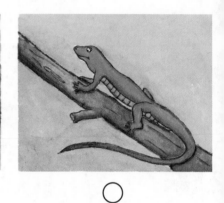

○ ○ ○

2 Which picture shows something that has been **snared**?

○ ○ ○

Teacher: Read aloud each numbered item and have children fill in the bubble under the best picture.

3 Which picture shows a bear cub being **nestled**?

○ ○ ○

4 Which picture shows a mouse **pouncing**?

○ ○ ○

5 Which picture shows something that is **unlikely**?

○ ○ ○

Listen. Draw.

1 solitude

2 sprinkle

Teacher: For each numbered item, read the vocabulary word aloud. Ask children to draw a line through the pictures that show the word in some way. Then ask children to tell why they connected the pictures they did.

Listen. Color. Draw.

muddle
expectation

Teacher: Ask children to color green the shirt of the boy who is in a **muddle**. Ask them to draw in the thought bubble the girl's **expectation** about the weather. Then ask children to tell which picture they colored, what they drew, and why.

51

1 Which picture shows someone **sprinkling** something?

○   ○   ○

2 Which picture shows a **muddle**?

○   ○   ○

Teacher: Read aloud each numbered item and have children fill in the bubble under the best picture.

3 Which picture shows **solitude**?

○   ○   ○

4 Which picture shows part of a **progression**?

○   ○   ○

5 Which picture shows a mouse with the **expectation** of a broken vase?

○   ○   ○

enormous

Petting
ZOO

Teacher: Direct children to the boy and his father at the top of the path and the girl and her mother at the bottom. Ask children to help the boy and father find the mother and sister by drawing a line through the animals that are **enormous**. Then ask children which pictures they drew a line through and why.

Listen. Draw.

sway

delighted

cooperate

struggle

Teacher: Ask children to look at the party scene and tell what they see. Then ask children to draw a circle around some flowers that are **swaying**. Then ask children to draw a wavy line under the kitten who is **delighted**. Have them draw a box around the kittens at the table who are **cooperating**. Have them draw a line under the kitten who is **struggling** to carry something. Ask children which pictures they marked and why.

1 Which picture shows an **enormous** balloon?

○ ○ ○

2 Which picture shows a mother **swaying** with her baby?

○ ○ ○

Teacher: Read aloud each numbered item and have children fill in the bubble under the best picture.

3 Which picture shows a **delighted** boy?

○ ○ ○

4 Which picture shows two children **cooperating**?

○ ○ ○

5 Which picture shows a man **struggling**?

○ ○ ○

flustered

slumber

plea

Teacher: Ask children to look at the park scene and tell what they see. Have them draw a line under the man who is **flustered**. Have them draw a box around the dog that is **slumbering**. Then ask them to draw a circle around someone who is making a **plea** for something. Ask children which pictures they marked and why.

Listen. Color.

1

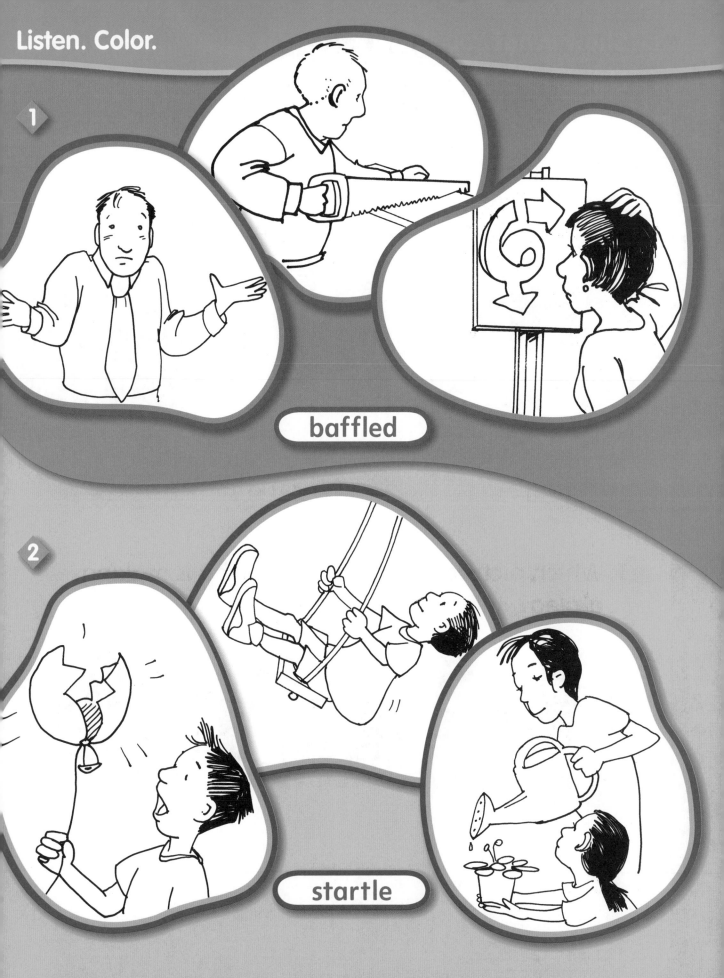

baffled

2

startle

Teacher: For each numbered item, read the vocabulary word aloud. Ask children to color the picture or pictures that match the word. Then ask children to tell which pictures they colored and why.

59

1 Which picture shows a bear that is slumbering?

○   ○   ○

2 Which picture shows someone who is making a plea?

○   ○   ○

Teacher: Read aloud each numbered item and have children fill in the bubble under the best picture.

3 What might **startle** someone?

○ ○ ○

4 Which picture shows someone who is **baffled**?

○ ○ ○

5 Which person is **flustered**?

○ ○ ○

creak

Teacher: Direct children's attention to the mouse at the top of the path and the group of mice near the bottom. Ask children to help the mouse find its friends by drawing a line through the things that **creak**. Then ask children to tell which pictures they drew a line through and why.

Listen. Draw.

1 stalk

2 action

Teacher: For each numbered item, read the vocabulary word aloud. Ask children to draw a line through the pictures that show the word in some way. Then ask children to tell why they connected the pictures they did.

63

1 Which picture shows **action**?

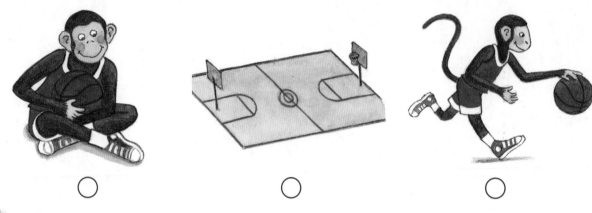

○   ○   ○

2 Which group is **chattering**?

○   ○   ○

Teacher: Read aloud each numbered item and have children fill in the bubble under the best picture.

3 Which picture shows an animal **stalking**?

◯   ◯   ◯

4 Which is the most likely to **creak**?

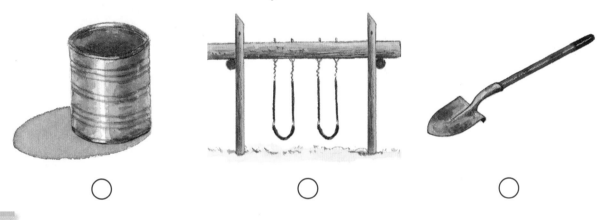

◯   ◯   ◯

5 Which cat is **communicating**?

◯   ◯   ◯

Listen. Color.

1 aware

2 scraggly

3 prod

Teacher: For each numbered item, read the vocabulary word aloud. Ask children to color the picture or pictures that match the word. Then ask children to tell which pictures they colored and why.

Listen. Color. Draw.

witty

plump

Teacher: Ask children to color blue the shirt of the person telling a **witty** story. Ask them to draw a funny hat on the clown who is **plump**. Then ask children to tell which shirt they colored, where they drew the hat, and why.

1 Which picture shows a camper **prodding** a campfire?

○   ○   ○

2 Which picture shows an **alert** puppy?

○   ○   ○

Teacher: Read aloud each numbered item and have children fill in the bubble under the best picture.

3 Which picture shows a **witty** actor?

◯ ◯ ◯

4 Which picture shows a **scraggly** cat?

◯ ◯ ◯

5 Which picture shows a **plump** pillow?

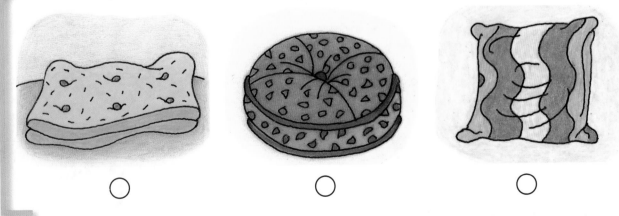

◯ ◯ ◯

1 entertain

2 gather

3 romp

Teacher: For each numbered item, read the vocabulary word aloud. Ask children to draw a line to connect pictures that show the same word. Then ask children to explain why they connected the pictures they did.

Listen. Draw.

creative

Teacher: Direct children to the boy at the top of the path and the theater door near the bottom. Ask children to help the boy find his way into the theater by drawing a line through the people who are **creative**. Then ask children to tell which pictures they drew a line through and why.

71

1 Which picture shows a dog wearing a **fad**?

○   ○   ○

2 Which picture shows animals **entertaining**?

○   ○   ○

Teacher: Read aloud each numbered item and have children fill in the bubble under the best picture.

3 In which picture is someone **gathering** something?

○   ○   ○

4 Which picture shows someone being **creative**?

○   ○   ○

5 Which picture shows a boy and dog **romping**?

○   ○   ○

Listen. Color.

hatch eager

slither

Teacher: Ask children to color blue the bird that is **hatching**. Ask them to color yellow the dog that is **eager**. Ask them to color green the animal that is **slithering**. Ask children to tell which pictures they colored and why.

Listen. Draw.

1 haven

2 hatch

Teacher: For each numbered item, read the vocabulary word aloud. Ask children to draw a line through the pictures that show the word in some way. Then ask children to tell why they connected the pictures they did.

75

1 Which picture shows **slime**?

○　　　　　○　　　　　○

2 Which animal is **slithering**?

○　　　　　○　　　　　○

3 Which picture shows an animal **hatching**?

○   ○   ○

4 Which picture shows an **eager** squirrel?

○   ○   ○

5 Which picture shows an animal's **haven**?

○   ○   ○

Listen. Draw.

survey
labor
beacon

Teacher: Ask children to look at the scene of a sailing ship from long ago and tell what they see. Ask them to draw a circle around the man who is **surveying** something. Have them draw a line under the sailor who is **laboring**. Have them draw a box around the **beacon**. Then ask children to tell which pictures they marked and why.

Listen. Color.

1

mammoth

2

memorable

Teacher: For each numbered item, read the vocabulary word aloud. Ask children to color the picture or pictures that match the word. Then ask children to tell which pictures they colored and why.

79

1 Which picture shows a man **laboring**?

    ◯   ◯   ◯

2 Which picture shows a girl seeing something **memorable**?

    ◯   ◯   ◯

Teacher: Read aloud each numbered item and have children fill in the bubble under the best picture.

3 Which picture shows a **mammoth** animal?

       ○   ○   ○

4 Which picture shows a boy who is **surveying**?

       ○   ○   ○

5 Which picture shows a **beacon**?

       ○   ○   ○

Listen. Color.

1 stroke

2 dive

3 yank

82

Teacher: For each numbered item, read the vocabulary word aloud. Ask children to color the picture or pictures that match the word. Then ask children to tell which pictures they colored and why.

Listen. Draw.

1 idle

2 task

3 dive

Teacher: For each numbered item, read the vocabulary word aloud. Ask children to draw a line to connect pictures that show the same word. Then ask children to explain why they connected the pictures they did.

83

1 Which picture shows a girl **stroking** an animal?

○   ○   ○

2 Which picture shows a seal **diving**?

○   ○   ○

Teacher: Read aloud each numbered item and have children fill in the bubble under the best picture.

3 Which picture shows a baby **yanking** something?

○ ○ ○

4 Which picture shows an **idle** skunk?

○ ○ ○

5 Which picture shows a skunk doing a **task**?

○ ○ ○

spin

Teacher: Direct children to the girl and her mother at the top of the path and the boy and father near the bottom. Ask children to help the mother and girl find the father and brother by drawing a line through the people or things that are **spinning**. Then ask children to tell which pictures they drew a line through and why.

Listen. Draw.

lovely
underneath
transform

Teacher: Ask children to look at the backyard scene and tell what they see. Ask them to draw a circle around someone who is wearing a **lovely** hat. Have them draw a box around the kitten that is **underneath** the chair. Ask them to draw a line under the thing in the sky that is about to **transform** the weather. Then ask children to tell which pictures they marked and why.

87

1 Which picture shows a dog hiding **underneath** something?

◯   ◯   ◯

2 Which picture shows a turtle holding something **lovely**?

◯   ◯   ◯

Teacher: Read aloud each numbered item and have children fill in the bubble under the best picture.

3 Which picture shows a mouse **spinning**?

○   ○   ○

4 Which picture shows something **transforming**?

○   ○   ○

5 Which picture shows the start of a **cycle**?

○   ○   ○

inquire
seek
swerve

Teacher: Ask children to look at the park scene and tell what they see. Then ask children to draw a circle around an animal that is **inquiring**. Have them draw a line under an animal that is **swerving** around a tree. Ask them to draw a box around an animal **seeking** a ball. Then ask children to tell which pictures they marked and why.

90

Listen. Draw.

mighty

Teacher: Direct children to the crocodile at the top of the path and the river near the bottom. Ask children to help the crocodile find the river by drawing a line through the animals that are **mighty**. Then ask children to tell which pictures they drew a line through and why.

1 Which picture shows a turtle **inquiring**?

○   ○   ○

2 Which picture shows a **swerving** horse?

○   ○   ○

Teacher: Read aloud each numbered item and have children fill in the bubble under the best picture.

3 Which picture shows a boat **drifting**?

○   ○   ○

4 Which picture shows a **mighty** tractor?

○   ○   ○

5 Which picture shows a bear **seeking** food?

○   ○   ○

Listen. Draw.

1 cramped

2 mimic

3 prowl

Teacher: For each numbered item, read the vocabulary word aloud. Ask children to draw a line to connect pictures that show the same word. Then ask children to tell which pictures they connected and why.

Listen. Color.

1

rhythm

2

dazzling

Teacher: For each numbered item, read the vocabulary word aloud. Ask children to color the picture or pictures that match the word. Then ask children to tell which pictures they colored and why.

95

1 Which picture shows a **cramped** dog?

○   ○   ○

2 Which picture shows a **dazzling** bird?

○   ○   ○

Teacher: Read aloud each numbered item and have children fill in the bubble under the best picture.

3 Which picture shows a **prowling** animal?

○ ○ ○

4 Which picture shows **rhythm**?

○ ○ ○

5 Which picture shows a dog **mimicking** a cat?

○ ○ ○

Words I Have Learned

A

absurd
action
active
adventure
alert
amble
ancient
appreciate
aware

B

baffled
bare
beacon
broad

C

celebrate
chatter
collide
comforting
communicate
cooperate
cramped
creak
creative
cycle

D

dazzling
delighted
describe

desire
discouraged
displeased
dive
drenched
drift

E

eager
enormous
entertain
expectation
expression
extraordinary

F

fad
fetch
fleet
flustered
frantic

G

gather
glance
glide
glimmer
gorgeous

H

hatch
haven
hefty
hesitate

I

idle
inquire
intimidated

J

journey

L

labor
linger
lively
lounge
lovely

M

mammoth
memorable
mighty
mimic
mischievous
muddle

N

narrow
nestle

O

observe
option

P

peculiar
perilous
plea
plump
pounce
prod
progression
prowl
pursue

R

relief
reluctant
request
respect
rhythm
roam
romp

S

scamper
scraggly
seek
slime
slither
slumber
snare
soar
solitude
spin
splendid
sprinkle
stalk
startle
stroke
struggle

stumble
survey
sway
swerve
swirl

T

task
timid
track
transform

U

underneath
unlikely

V

vain
village

W

wavy
whisk
witty

Y

yank

99

My Favorite Words

Teacher: Invite children to tell favorite words they have learned. Ask them to explain why these words are favorites—are they fun to say, are there lots of times when they can use them, or do they just make them happy? Then help children write the words on this list. Encourage children to add to their lists as they learn to use new words, both in and out of the classroom.